ALL MEN
ARE TRASH

Gina Ranalli

Madness Heart Press
2006 Idlewilde Run Dr.
Austin, Texas 78744

Cover by John Baltisberger

First Edition
www.madnessheart.press

Dedication:

For every woman who has ever roared in protest, whether with her voice or only in her heart. Stay strong. Stay dangerous. I love you.

Acknowledgments:

Infinite thanks to Jeff Burk, without whom this book would not exist, Lucas Mangum, for pointing me in the perfect direction, Christine Morgan, one of the most outstanding editors a writer could ever hope to work with and of course, John Baltisberger, for his enthusiasm for and belief in this project. And lastly, thank you, readers. Your support will always be the best part of this crazy job.

1

His father, a massive fan of the horror genre, both movies and books, had named him Bram and despite other children making fun of him during his youth, Bram March wore his name with pride and had never resented it, most likely because he'd always been the apple of his father's eye. Being hyper masculine didn't hurt either. The first and only time he'd ever come home from school crying as a result of the teasing, his dad had advised him to sucker punch the kid the next time he said anything nasty. Skeptical, Bram had not taken his father's advice, but when questioned about it the next day, when asked if he'd hit the kid, his dad had been so disgusted with Bram the day after *that*, he'd done as instructed. He'd been dragged into the principal's office, true, but when his father came to the school to discuss the matter, he'd been beaming and Bram had grinned along with him, so much so that he'd gone on to assault virtually every other boy who'd said anything disparaging about him, until the insults had stopped. True, he'd been expelled several times, a fact his mother was not pleased with, but Bram didn't much care for her opinion anyway. It was his dad whose approval mattered.

Aside from the fights, which grew less frequent the older Bram got, school hadn't been the best use of his time. Fighting accomplished something algebra and *Moby Dick* did not. He'd been a decent student, doing what needed to be done to graduate, but he'd had no desire to go on to college. Instead, with the blessing of his dad, Bram had joined the US Coast Guard, a truly miserable experience for him. He'd thought the discipline would be invigorating but in truth, he'd resented being pushed around by his superiors, particularly the eight weeks of basic training he'd endured. Once he'd finally done his three years, he was out. The military life was not for him and so, he'd followed in his father's footsteps and gone to work as a construction contractor, a job that paid well and he excelled at. He was currently celebrating his first decade in the field and was expecting to do the same work until the day he died, like his father who'd literally died on site several years before.

At thirty-two, Bram was having to contend with life without his hero, but he was managing, as men had to. When he'd been twenty-five, he'd almost had to get married, due to an unexpected and, on his part, completely unwanted, pregnancy, but he avoided that particular train wreck by demanding the young woman—only eighteen—have an abortion. It hadn't been easy, but he knew she was trying to trap him and he'd have none of that bullshit. After much cajoling, she'd seen the situation his way and done what needed doing, thank Jesus.

He'd wanted his freedom and he'd be damned if he wasn't going to get it. When the same thing had happened to his best friend Fulton, Bram had encouraged him to do exactly what he had done: tell the girl she wasn't the only one he'd been fucking. It was the quickest and easiest way to get a chick off your back. It just so happened that in Bram's case it was true. Fulton, on the other hand, claimed to love the woman, had married her and now had three snot-nosed brats running around. Bram now insisted when they got together, Fulton came to his house instead. The kids drove Bram nuts.

Bram and Fulton had been friends since grade school, fourth grade, to be exact, so Fulton knew everything there was to know about Bram. He'd seen the fist fights, listened to Bram bitch about his military service while also praising his dad for being such a great role model. Fulton, too, had been bullied a great deal for the same reason—an unusual first name—but he'd mostly laughed it off. His nature was far easier than Bram's, making them a bit of an odd pairing but still, they'd been best friends ever since, even working together more often than not.

Currently stuck in afternoon traffic, it was Fulton who Bram decided to call on his cellphone, out of sheer boredom. Fulton's phone went straight to voicemail, the outgoing message being only two words: "Leave it."

"Yeah, I'll leave it," Bram said. "Under my ball sack." He laughed heartily at his own joke. "Just kidding, man. Stuck in traffic, thought I'd say what's up. Call me when you get this."

He ended the call and tossed the phone onto the passenger seat, staring at the ass end of a pick-up with a pro Hilary Clinton bumper sticker, faded and peeling at the corners. Bram snorted, wondering if a chick was behind the wheel or if some poor sap was driving around with his wife's political fantasies on display to embarrass him. Either way, Bram resolved to flip the truck driver off if he had the opportunity to pass. The driver would probably be puzzled but Bram didn't care. His own truck, a newer black Ford Trinidad, didn't sport any stickers but if it had, they would have been red and white, like every other sensible American. Of course, sensible Americans were a rare commodity these days, but that was okay. Order was being restored, slowly but surely. Soon all the snowflakes would be melted away by the flames of righteousness and the United States could get back to the business of making money and putting certain sects of people right where they belonged. Bram had all the faith in the world things would be set right at last.

Behind him, a yuppie in a Volkswagen tooted his little fairy horn impatiently. It sounded like a toy. Bram scowled in his rearview mirror, hoping to send a message with just his eyes, but he wasn't much irritated. His mood was good, as he pondered the sirloin steak in his freezer and the case of Bud on the flooboard in front of the passenger seat. It was Thursday night, almost the weekend and he looked forward to sleeping in, not getting dirt beneath his nails or sweating through his T-shirt for a couple days.

He didn't think the guy in the Volkswagen was paying him any attention so his adjusted the mirror to look at himself instead, brown eyes so dark they could be mistaken for black, staring briefly at his full Dallas mustache, which he ran his index finger and thumb across quickly, as was a habit of his, keeping it as neat as possible. He wore a dark blue ballcap, forward while he was driving but always backwards otherwise, the Seattle Sawfish logo emblazoned across the front of it. Satisfied with the state of his stache, he adjusted the mirror back to its previous position and reached into the breast pocket of his flannel shirt, pulling out a stick of spearmint gum. He put the wrapping back in his pocket so as not to litter in the truck and chewed thoughtfully. The radio was on, almost too low to hear, tuned to a news station, but he doubted they were saying anything of interest to him.

Finally, the traffic began to move again. He'd be home before six with any luck, hopefully while there was still a little light left in the sky. Soon it would be spring, which meant more daylight, but longer hours spent at construction sites. T-shirts instead of flannels would be nice though. He was pondering this when his cell chimed, and he snatched it up assuming it would be Fulton returning his call but was surprised to see a number he didn't recognize. He smiled. Unlike most people, who ignored unknown numbers, he delighted in them. Any chance to give a telemarketer grief was a good time in his book. He answered in a cheery voice. "Hello?"

"Mr. March?"

A woman's voice.

"Who's calling?" He really wanted it to be a bullshit call. Playing with her would alleviate his boredom for a couple minutes.

"My name is Emma Ames. I'm calling to ask if you've had a chance to review my application."

So much for alleviating the boredom. Bram said nothing. His attention was caught by a pretty blonde driving a red convertible Palomino.

Emma Ames cleared her throat. "I sent my resume to you three weeks ago and was assured I'd hear back in two."

"Ah," Bram said. "Well, I guess we decided to go with someone else. Sorry about that but thanks for calling."

He was about to end the call when she quickly said, "Can I ask why?"

"Why what?"

"Why you went with someone else?"

Bram chuckled. "Probably because they were more qualified." There was silence on the other end. "Anything else?"

"I find that hard to believe," she said.

His eyebrows shot up. This might be fun after all. "Is that right?"

"Actually, I think your company is known for its gender bias."

"What?"

"I've been doing research and discovered you haven't hired a single woman in all your years of operation."

Bram's amusement quickly turned into annoyance. "Well, that's bullshit."

"No, it's actually not. I've—"

"How did you get this number?"

"I googled you."

"This is my private, personal number."

"Like I said—"

"Don't call me again. If you have any issues, I suggest you take it up with the HR department."

"As far as I can tell, you don't have an HR department."

"Goodbye."

Bram ended the call before the bitch could say anything else. What the fuck? Emma something. He'd already forgotten her last name but he took his eyes off the road briefly to block the number on his phone.

It was in that split second that traffic slowed drastically and his truck plowed into the rear-end of the red Palomino, which had changed lanes a moment before.

Metal crunched and glass shattered as he stomped the brake, too late.

A quick assessment told him he was fine. He looked up to see the blonde in the red car, still moving, so obviously she was unhurt as well, thank Jesus. They hadn't been moving more than 30 mph. Again, thank Jesus.

He exited the truck and went to her, just to be sure. The back of her car was damaged but it probably wasn't totaled.

As he approached the driver's side of the vehicle, he called, "Are you okay?"

Traffic began moving again, the drivers jaded and impatient, moving around the accident without bothering to stop and check if anyone needed help.

Bram saw their faces, both pale and dark, glance at him as they passed, maybe hoping for a little blood but seeing none, speeding on into their evenings.

"I'm fine," the woman said. "At least I think so."

She didn't seem hurt. She was wearing her seatbelt.

"Let's get off the road," he said and she nodded.

He gave the front of his truck a cursory glance and saw it was mostly okay. Dinged and scratched but it sat high enough off the ground so the headlights were fine. He thanked Jesus one more time as he climbed in, cursing his shitty luck—his steak, beer and enthusiasm for home forgotten.

*

The woman Bram had rear-ended was named Claire Hill. They both stood on the side of the freeway assessing the damage to her car and exchanging their information. Bram tried to not stare at Claire's tits, but she was wearing a red tank-top and it was a challenge. She also wore too-tight jeans and cowboy boots. She was hot, her blonde hair spilling over her shoulders in shiny cascades of gold. On the road, the passing cars were just starting to turn on their headlights as darkness began to fall.

Bram cleared his throat. "Uh . . . aren't you cold? You want to get a jacket or something?" The woman's nipples poked provocatively through the fabric of the top.

"I'm fine," she said, looking down at the paper

he'd handed her, scrawled with his name, number and insurance info. "Bram, huh? There's a name you don't hear every day."

"Yeah." He pulled his eyes from her chest, wondering how she couldn't be cold. The temperature was only in the mid-thirties. He glanced at her car again, with its top dropped, then back at her face, which was almost as pretty as her tits. "Anyway," he said. "Your car seems drivable but if you want me to wait with you while you call a tow, I will." He didn't want to but he figured it was the polite thing to do. He was starting to think about the accident itself, hoping he wasn't gonna get too screwed over by his insurance company. Or hers. He didn't think the flow of traffic had slowed to such a degree that she'd been forced to slam on her brakes the way she had but maybe she was a nervous driver. Whatever the case, he knew the accident wasn't his fault.

Instead of answering his question, she said, "Actually, do you have a phone I could borrow?"

"Oh. Uh, sure." He patted his pockets. "Hang on. It's in the truck."

As he walked back to the pickup, he snuck a peek over his shoulder at her. She smiled, staring at him. He wondered if she was flirting and thought it could be possible. He was a decent looking guy, in better-than-average shape and he clearly had enough money for one of the newest Trinidads on the market. He smiled back as he opened the truck door to the sound of his phone chiming in the cab. He climbed inside, locating the phone on the floorboard in front of the case of beer. He hadn't gotten to it fast enough. It had already switched over to voicemail. He sat behind the wheel, checked the recently received calls and saw another number he didn't recognize. Somewhat annoyed, he got out and went back to Claire who was now leaning against the back of her car, arms folded across her mid-section. Even in the gloom, Bram could see goosebumps on her arms. He outstretched his hand, offering her the cellphone. It rang again before he could hand it over.

He frowned, said "sorry' and glanced at it again. The same number. *What the hell?* He held up his free index finger to Claire and turned slightly away from her as he answered it.

"Hi, Bram," a familiar voice said. "It's me again. She paused. "Emma." Another pause. "From before."

How many numbers did this bitch have, he wondered. He kept his voice quiet as he said, "Do you think harassing me is gonna get you a job, lady?"

"Maybe," she replied, sounding amused now. "At least it might once I tell you you're going to be sued."

"Excuse me?" He felt his anger rising. "For what?"

"Discrimination, what do you think?"

He almost argued. Almost protested. But at the last instant, he hung up on her instead. His blood pressure didn't need this shit right now. Once more,

14

he turned back to Claire. "Sorry about that."

"Everything okay?" she asked.

"Uh . . . yeah, fine."

"You don't look like everything is fine."

"Just . . . " He shook his head. "Pesky gnat," he said, finally. "No big deal." He handed her the phone. She accepted it, walking away from him as she dialed. He sighed, shoving his hands into the pockets of his jeans, shivering, leaning against the front of his truck. He looked at her ass with appreciation for a moment, imagined grabbing it while she rode him, those beautiful, bountiful tits swinging above his face. Then he glanced at the traffic whizzing by and wished he was one of those drivers, almost home. He was suddenly tired. More tired than he had a right to be, really. It had been an easy day. Twelve hours long now, sure, but easy nonetheless.

The Palomino's engine roared and he looked over, blinking in surprise, expecting her to peel out and take off. Instead, Claire threw the car into reverse and stomped on the gas, the tires spitting dirt and gravel as she plowed the Palomino into both the Trinidad and Bram, trapping him between the two.

Bram screamed, a sound that was lost, at least to his own ears, as the car crushed one of his legs, snapping it.

The woman pulled forward and Bram crumpled to the ground, shrieking, holding his thigh with both hands as the woman sped away into the night.

2

Nicki snapped her gum under the harsh fluorescents of the Solar Pharmaceutical ceiling. She stood at the register checking her phone, waiting for the next customer to come along to be checked out. The store was dead and she was almost bored enough to ask Mike, her manager, if she could leave the confines of the register and do something on the floor, even if it was just facing off the aisles or some stupid shit. He wouldn't allow it, of course. There was a customer in the store, slowly moving his way around, seeming to check the price of every item the store carried, judging by the amount of time he'd been there, which seemed like forever to Nicki.

Whatever, though. She'd happily get paid for just standing around, checking social media, which was

16

probably what she'd be doing if she was at home anyway. But at least she'd be relaxing on her bed. Her feet were beginning to ache and she still had three hours to go before the end of her shift. A snack would be nice too.

Luckily, or maybe unluckily, a few minutes later, customers began drifting into the store. Just a few. An older straight couple holding hands and a younger woman with a butterfly tattooed on her left temple. Nicki smiled at each of them, said hello, all the usual shit, then went back to frowning at her phone once they were out of sight, disappeared into the bowels of the store, most of them probably headed for the now-closed pharmacy at the back. She expected to hear complaining soon enough.

She was reading the comments on a yet another enraging news story when the first customer—the one who'd roamed aimlessly for what seemed like forever—approached the counter. He was a younger guy, probably early twenties, like herself, a bit on the pudgy side, also like herself, dressed like a stereotypical nerd, completely unlike herself.

He held up a box of condoms for her to observe. "I need extra-large."

Nicki sucked in her right cheek, placing the flesh between her teeth for a moment, not responding.

The guy raised both his hands and eyebrows at her, as if to say, *Well?*

She raised her own eyebrows back at him before

resuming her gum chewing.

"I didn't see any," he said.

"They should be there."

"I didn't see any."

"Did you check the top shelf? That's where they are."

"Yeah, I checked. There weren't any."

Resisting the urge to sigh, she said, "I can call my manager."

"Why? Can't you just . . . like . . . check the back room or whatever?"

"No," she replied. "I'm the only register open. I can't leave the front."

"But there's no one else in line."

As if on cue, the older couple came up and stood behind the pudgy young guy. Nicki gestured at them. "There is now."

The guy's apple cheeks flushed deeper. "Oh, come on," he said after a moment. He stared at her, clearly annoyed.

"You sure you don't want me to call the manager?"

The girl with the tattooed face joined the line and it was her turn to earn the ire of the chubby guy with the supposedly huge dick. He glanced back and forth, shooting everyone daggers. At last, he said, "Fine, I'll just get these."

Nicki shrugged and held out her hand to ring up his purchase. He gave her the condoms, then said,

"Shit! I forgot something."

She bit the inside of her cheek again, resisting the urge to ask if he forgot the lube. The girl with the tattoo groaned and the older couple exchanged a glance. Chub boy dropped the condoms on the counter and said, "I'll be right back."

Nicki was usually indifferent to the customers, regardless of their attitudes, but right then and there she didn't like this guy and she decided not to appease him. "No problem, but you can get to the back of the line when you come back."

He froze, glaring. "What?"

"Sorry. Other customers." She lifted her chin in their direction.

"That's bullshit."

"It's rude to make them wait. You've already been in this store for like, half an hour. At least."

"So what?"

"So nothing. What's the big deal? By the time you're done shuffling around the store like Eeyore, they'll be gone anyway."

"No, I know what I want. I just gotta . . . " He trailed off, his face clouding with anger. "What did you just say to me?"

"You have to go to the back of the line if you step out of it."

He pointed a finger at her. "That's bullshit *and* you just insulted me."

Nicki snapped her gum and gazed back at him,

hiding her own annoyance with a bored expression.

"Call your fucking manager," he ordered.

Without saying a word, she lifted the phone and called for Mike to come to register 7. It took him a minute to arrive because, she knew, he'd been re-stocking the coolers in the back. During that minute, the other customers shifted uncomfortably. Nicki felt a bit bad for them. They had no choice but to just stand there, witnessing this hostile encounter. For her part, she wasn't uncomfortable at all. In fact, she was doing her best to suppress a certain amount of glee. This guy was being an absolute dick and she was tired of customers—guys, in particular—being assholes to her. Giving one some grief—even a small quantity—felt amazingly good.

Mike arrived and before Nicki could even open her mouth, fat boy started in, ranting and raving, saying she'd called him Eeyore, the whole nine, at which point Mike gave her a look like he'd never heard of anything so shocking in his whole life. She resisted the temptation to roll her eyes.

When the douchebag was finally finished with his story of blatant abuse at the hands of a lowly ca-shier, Mike was very apologetic and escorted him back to where they stocked the condoms, informing Nicki that she was indeed going to hold the line up and wait for their return.

Nicki couldn't believe it but held her tongue until they were out of earshot. Once they were, she looked at the other customers. "Really sorry about this, guys. What an ass clown, huh?" The older couple said nothing, looking away, probably embarrassed by the entire scene while the tattooed girl held Nicki's gaze and gave her a small, maybe sympathetic smile. Nicki couldn't really tell.

When Mike returned with Fuckface in tow, she saw the new box of condoms in his hand. She smirked at the chubby guy. "Told you they were there."

"Yeah, whatever." He practically threw the box at her. She rang him up without speaking until having to ask if he wanted a bag. Mike stood there the whole time, arms folded across his middle-aged belly, looking somewhat like a suburban Buddha.

As the customer turned to leave, in her sweetest most sarcastic voice, Nicki said, "Have a *great* evening, sir."

The guy looked at her with pure hatred, replied with an equal amount of sarcasm. *"You too. Bitch."*

Mike was gaping at her, a look on his face that said, *oh, we are gonna have words, you and I.*

She couldn't agree with that sentiment any more. They would have words all right.

Mike walked away, and Nicki continued checking out the rest of the customers. The remainder of her shift was uneventful until she went to clock out and say goodnight to Mike. Normally, she would have offered to help him close, but not tonight. Fuck that.

21

She found him in the back, loading the coolers with new bottles of champagne and this annoyed her further. If she had taken two plus hours for that particular task, he would have bitched her out. She suspected he'd been fucking around, probably playing Candy Crush or some shit.

"I'm out of here," she told him.

"Hold up," he said, turning away from the cooler to face her. "I want to talk to you about what happened earlier."

She regarded him coolly. "So talk."

"Your attitude with that customer was uncalled for."

"I disagree. You weren't there. My attitude was totally called for."

He stared at her for along moment. "I have to tell you, Nicki, you're skating on thin ice."

"Yeah, okay." She dropped her gaze to the half empty box of champagne, suddenly thirsty. "Whatever."

"That's exactly what I'm talking about. That terrible attitude." When she didn't reply, he added, "And I've asked you numerous times to stop chewing gum while you're on register."

"No problem," she said and grabbed a bottle of champagne. "I'm gonna grab one of these, okay? Seems like a night for celebration."

"Can you please listen to—"

Gripping the heavy bottle in both hands, she

swung it at his head as hard as she could. His skull cracked and he went down instantly. She was surprised the bottle didn't break. "I'm listening," she said. "Was there anything else you wanted to say?"

Mike was out—either unconscious or dead, blood matting what little hair he had on the right side of his head and starting to trickle onto the linoleum floor beneath it.

"No?" she asked. "We're good then? Okay. Have a good one."

On her way out of the store, she spit her gum at the register as she passed, bottle in hand and wondered if anything interesting was happening online.

3

About an hour after Mark Gray had finished fucking his wife, fifty minutes after his shower, he was sitting up in bed, reading a Tom Clancy novel. Patti was beside him, on her phone, doing he didn't care what. He pushed his reading glasses up on his nose and turned a page, fully engrossed in the story. He heard Patti sigh, but didn't question it. She sighed a lot these days and he knew from experience the sigh usually meant something she'd read or seen had irritated her and if he asked, he was apt to get an earful he didn't want or need. Best to ignore it and mind his own business. There was a good chance he'd have to hear about her latest aggravation anyway. No sense in rushing it or even provoking it on the off chance she might spare him.

His hopes for peace were dashed almost immediately. She said, "I cannot believe this fucking shit."

Without looking away from his book, he asked, "What shit?"

"Another piece of shit college punk getting away with rape."

Inwardly, Mark winced. Not this one again. But what he said was, "Oh, Jesus. You've got to be kidding me."

"Little rich white fuckers. They're just monsters and their scumbag parents buying scumbag judges ought to go to prison right along with them. The whole lot of them need to be put away."

"You can say that again," Mark agreed, but hoped she wouldn't take his statement to heart.

"And you know what kind of message this sends to all the other little pricks running around? It says 'do whatever you want, boys. We'll always have your backs because you possess penises, which somehow makes you so much more valuable than the people who possess vaginas! Let's all just high-five each other!"

Mark dared a glance at her. She was really working herself into a frenzy this time.

"Take a breath, hon," he said. "No sense in raising your blood pressure about this shit."

She put her phone down and faced him. "Well, someone's blood pressure needs to be raised about it. Clearly, someone—a *lot* of *someones*—need to put their feet down and say enough is enough."

Oh, fuck, he thought, closing his book on his lap to look at her. They'd been married for two and a half decades, mostly happily. They'd raised two kids, a girl and a boy, both currently away at college. Patti was not an unreasonable woman. She was intelligent and kind, firm in her beliefs of right and wrong. It was only in the last couple years that she'd been . . . he supposed the word would be *moody*.

"Don't give me that look," she said.

He lowered the reading glasses further down the bridge of his nose. "What look?"

"That, *oh, great, here she goes again*, look."

"I wasn't giving you a look."

"You were thinking it."

"I wasn't thinking anything." Her apparent telepathy was unnerving but he held his ground. "You're getting worked up over nothing."

"Nothing?" Her voice was rising. "How can you say this news is *nothing?* It's rampant! And have you forgotten we have a daughter in college?"

"Of course not. But, Becca's not like that."

He could tell immediately he'd stepped in it now. Her blue eyes blazing, she snapped, "Like *that*? Like *what*, exactly, *Mark*?"

Trying desperately to think of a way out of this one, he wasn't quick enough.

"A *slut*? Is that what you're implying by that remark? That only *sluts* get raped? That boys would never behave the way they do if it wasn't for the *sluts* who tempt them?"

"*What?*" He was offended now. "Absolutely not! Where is this coming from?"

She snatched her phone up and waved it in his face. "Right here! In the comments section. Man after man, spouting the same bullshit over and over. Would you like me to read them to you?"

"No, I really wouldn't." He had to think of a way to calm her down. He gave her a coy smile and reached out, stroking her thigh. "What do you say to round two?"

She blinked. "Excuse me?"

"You know, to relax you."

"That relaxes *you*, Mark. For Christ's sake! Don't pretend you ever put out for *me*!"

"I . . . " He stammered, beginning to feel the first twinges of anger now. But he couldn't snap back at her. That would set in motion a huge fight that could very well last for days, with the way she'd been lately. He bit back any snide comment he might otherwise have said and continued to smile. "I'll do . . . you know." He made a point of staring at her crotch and licked his lips.

"Are you fucking kidding me right now?"

Shit. His smile slid away as he braced himself for impact.

"And when was the last time you did *that?* Five

years? *Ten*?"

"Oh, come on! It hasn't been that long!"

"It most certainly has! And even when you deigned yourself to suffer through that particular indignity, you acted like you were God's precious gift to the clitoris and I hate to break it to you, but you're no Casanova, buddy."

He bristled. "What the hell is that supposed to mean?"

"You could barely find it! When you did, it was because I had to grab you by the fucking ears and steer you!"

"Patti!"

"It's true! You've never given a shit about my needs. Hell, you don't even touch me unless it's my crotch or my tits! Not to mention, you stopped even *kissing* me after Joey was born!"

"I kiss you all the time!"

"Not like you used to. But why would you? That might constitute *foreplay*, god fucking forbid."

"Okay." He took off his glasses and placed them and his book on the night table. "I'm not going to continue this. I didn't do anything wrong."

"Of course not! *Men* never do *anything* wrong!"

He turned out the lamp on his side. "I'm going to sleep now."

"Sure! Why not? Anything to shut up the little woman, right? I'm being *unreasonable*?"

"Yes, you actually are. You've lost your goddamn

mind!"

"*Fuck you!*" she shrieked, simultaneously punching him in the face.

He gasped in pain, cupping his hands over his nose, his eyes wide with shock as blood flowed from between his fingers. "You broke my fucking nose!"

"*Good!*" She threw the covers off herself and got out of bed, heading into the bathroom. She slammed the door, leaving him alone, blood dripping onto his bare chest and tears of agony streaming down his cheeks. He couldn't believe it. Neither of them had even been physically violent with either each other or their children. There had always been a 'no hitting' rule in the house, regardless of what was happening. They'd established it when the kids were little. Now he was furious, his heart slamming. His entire body was trembling, but he didn't think it was rage shaking him. It was hurt. He felt completely heartbroken and realized he might cry for real. Had he really said something so awful? He didn't think so.

He wanted to get out of bed, but didn't want to touch anything with his bloody hands or drip blood anywhere. He needed help.

"Patti," he called, his voice sounding odd in his own head, probably due to the broken nose. "Can you bring me a towel, please? I'm bleeding pretty bad out here."

A drawer slammed from behind the bathroom door, followed by a long pause.

"Honey?" he called.

The door flung open with enough force to slam it into the wall behind it and Patti lunged out, charging across the room towards him, a crazed look on her face, a small pair of trim scissors in her hand.

Mark was so stunned, he barely had time to react, throwing his arms up over his head and screeching in terror as his wife proceeded to stab him repeatedly in the stomach and chest.

The pain was unbearable but even in his shock and agony, he did his best to defend himself, first attempting to grab at her wrists and then punch her.

They were both screaming as they fought, him for what he thought was his life and her in murderous rage. It was only when his fist connected to her jaw and she was knocked back that she finally gave up, recovering quickly and then racing from the bedroom and down the stairs.

Mark was freely crying, looking down at his body and its many puncture wounds, shock already setting in. It was a full two minutes before it occurred to him to call 911.

4

Ariana Cruz sat in a Denny's booth a little after 7am the following morning, her hands wrapped around a hot mug filled with subpar coffee. She already knew she would be ordering a veggie omelet but was waiting for her girlfriend Jaclyn to arrive. A notebook lay open on the table before her, as she was trying to brainstorm ideas for a novel she wanted to write, but the straight couple behind her were having a very vocal argument, making it impossible to concentrate. Instead of brainstorming, she gazed out the window at the parking lot and the passing traffic on the main drag, unable to tune out the things the couple were saying.

"I don't know why you're being such a bitch," the man said.

"You think I'm being a bitch now," the woman snarled. "You just wait till we get home, you pompous asshole."

"You know what, Darlene? Fuck you. I can't deal with all this fucking drama anymore. If you want to leave because I'm such an asshole, then just do it."

"You moved in with me! *You* move out!"

"Yeah, you'd like that wouldn't you? Then you get to tell everyone I *abandoned* you, just like you did last time!"

Ariana was more than a little relieved when she saw Jaclyn enter the restaurant, spotting her right away and walking towards the booth with a smile. The fighting couple was merely background noise now as Ariana stood, greeting her girlfriend with a kiss.

"Sorry for being late," Jaclyn said as they sat, Ariana closing the notebook and setting it aside.

"No worries," she said. "I've only been here a few minutes."

They held hands across the table, smiling at each other. Their relationship was still young—not quite a year old—but Ariana was convinced Jaclyn was the one. Someday soon, she would ask Jac to move in with her.

Behind Ariana, the woman said, "Oh, here we go. Back to your gaslighting bullshit."

"I'm not gaslighting, Darlene! It *never happened*!"

Jaclyn looked past Ariana, frowning slightly before giving Ariana a questioning look. Ariana shrugged and rolled her eyes. Keeping her voice down, she leaned forward and said, "They've been at it for a while."

"We should change tables," Jaclyn said, looking around for the server. "This place is really dead this morning."

It was true. Only four tables, including their own, were occupied, which was unusual for this time of day. Not even the grayheads were out this morning.

"I definitely could use some coffee," Jaclyn said, snagging Ariana's mug for a sip.

Ariana grinned. "Please. Help yourself."

"Ew. Too much sugar."

"Not enough to make it taste better than sludge."

"*Fuck*!" The man in the neighboring booth yelled, startling both women. He jumped out of the booth suddenly, his face dripping with orange juice, the top of his button-down shirt drenched. "*You fucking bitch!*"

Now the fighting couple had the attention of everyone in the restaurant, including the staff.

"Fuck you!" the woman screamed, also getting out of the booth.

A young woman, presumably the manager, approached them quickly, her face strained. "I'm sorry, but—"

The man was already reaching for his wallet. "Yeah, I'm fucking leaving. Don't worry about it."

He tossed a collection of bills at the woman as he stormed towards the exit. The woman he was with gave chase and then they were out the door, still screaming at each other. Once they were gone, a few people in the restaurant chuckled nervously while the manager collected the money up from the floor.

Ariana watched the couple cross the parking lot, headed towards a minivan. The woman, who strode quickly to catch up to the man suddenly leapt at him, wrapping one arm around his neck while pummeling him with her free fist.

"Oh my god," Ariana said. "She's actually beating on him."

Jaclyn looked out. "Whoa."

The manager, who still stood by their booth, also saw the assault taking place in her parking lot. The man tried to wrestle himself away from the woman, but she held on. Even inside, everyone could still hear their screaming.

The manager walked briskly to the front of the restaurant by the register and picked up the phone. Momentarily, it became obvious she was calling the police.

"Well, this is nuts," Jaclyn said.

"Think we should do something?" Ariana asked, grimacing as she watched the couple struggling with each other.

"I don't know. They both seem crazy. Probably best to keep our distance. Unless you're craving a black eye?" She smiled as she said the last.

"Umm. Nah. Not today."

Outside, the man freed himself from the woman and somehow succeeded in getting inside the vehicle. The woman fought to prevent him from closing the door, but he eventually did, locking her out in the process. The woman began kicking the minivan, shrieking obscenities as he drove away. She took off running after him.

"Wow," Ariana said when they were out of sight. "You don't see that every day."

"Yeah, if you're lucky."

The server finally came over and took their meal orders, bringing Jaclyn her coffee a minute later.

After a sip, Jaclyn asked, "How's your self-imposed abstinence from the internet going?"

"It's going great. Almost seven whole days, so far."

"No withdrawals?"

"Not really. The first couple days were weird, forcing myself to not check my phone immediately. It was a reflex for so long, but now it's fine. How's it going for you?"

"Okay. I still can't believe I let you talk me into it."

"Yeah, well, I'm nothing if not a fantastic influence." She reached for Jaclyn's hand again. "Before you know it, I'll have you eating vegan at every meal."

Jaclyn laughed. "Don't push it, weirdo."

"So, no cheating? You deleted the apps from your phone?"

"Yes, ma'am. I still check the news, but only a couple times a day."

"And you're okay with that?"

"I mean, the news still sucks, all day, every day." She laughed again. One of Ariana's favorite things about Jaclyn was her quickness to laugh. "But that just makes it easier to not want to check it."

"Good. I'm proud of you."

Jaclyn squeezed her hand. "Oh, yeah? How proud?"

Ariana narrowed her eyes with suspicion, but she was still smiling. "Very proud."

"Proud enough to give me a reward?"

"What did you have in mind?"

Pretending to think about it for a few seconds, Jaclyn gazed off into space. When their eyes met again, hers were sparkling with mischief. "How about a shared shower, for starters?"

Before Ariana could reply, the server arrived with their food.

"Here you are, ladies. Need anything else?"

Ariana blushed slightly but said, "No, thanks. We're good."

"Enjoy your meals."

Reluctantly, they released each other's hands in favor of cutlery and napkins.

On the other side of the dining area, another straight couple began to argue.

5

Bram awoke in a hospital, adequately drugged, he supposed, given his condition. He didn't remember much about the previous evening but what he did remember, he wished he didn't.

His head hurt, he felt queasy but his legs . . . he didn't feel those at all. His hips ached though, and he supposed that had to do with radiating pain. Both his legs were in bad shape. He'd had emergency surgery. He remembered being told that at some point, and that he might still require another. Maybe more than just one. He also had a vague recollection of talking to cops at some point. He thought the sun had been up then but maybe it hadn't been the sun at all. He was confused and scared and all he could remember of the accident was a red sports car and the

38

name Claire. He thought now that that hadn't been her name at all. Just a feeling.

He closed his eyes, tried to drift, and he must have succeeded because he was startled when he heard movement near his head.

A nurse stood beside the bed. He smiled at Bram when he noticed his eyes open. "How are you feeling, Bram?" Without waiting for an answer, he asked, "Think you might be up for getting something in your stomach?" Again, without a reply, he held a plastic cup with a straw up to Bram's mouth. Bram drank dutifully.

"Great," the nurse said. "We'll see how that sits. Maybe get you graduated to ice chips in half an hour or so. How does that sound?"

"Good," Bram said, though he wasn't so sure. His stomach was still roiling. "I have a headache."

"I'm not surprised." The guy didn't seem all that concerned or even interested. He busied himself with checking the machines Bram was attached to. "Everything looks good here. I'll be back in a few with your ice."

Alone again, Bram tried to focus on the whiteboard on the wall opposite the bed. Apparently, his nurse was named John and he was on duty till 8pm. Bram had no idea what time it was now but judging by the light filtered in through the closed blinds, he guessed late morning or early afternoon. He'd be with John for a while yet.

He took a moment to examine what he could of himself. He wasn't yet brave enough to peek under the covers at his ruined legs, but his arms and hands seemed to be mostly okay. The ring finger on his left hand was splinted—he assumed broken—and he had some bruises and abrasions but overall, nothing too bad. No stitches anyway. He supposed in that one small regard, he'd been lucky. He felt his head, discovered bandages and tender spots that hurt when he prodded them. He quickly dropped his hands and opted not to ponder those injuries too much but assumed he'd discovered the reason for his headache.

Exploring the inside of his mouth with his tongue, everything seemed to be fine in there, with the exception of dryness. With effort, he leaned his upper body to the right and was able to reach the water cup the nurse had left. He sipped again, carefully at first, then drank normally, finishing half the cup in seconds. The water seemed to settle his stomach a bit, offering him at least a little relief from his overall discomfort.

What the fuck had been that bitch's problem last night? She'd just gone psycho on him, all of a sudden, without reason. He hoped the cops found her soon. He would get the best lawyer he could find and sue every damn person she'd ever known—get her put away forever.

He couldn't believe he'd been the victim of a random act of violence. Perpetrated by a woman, no less.

He tried to remember the last time he'd heard about something like this and nothing came to him. All he could think of from recent news stories were women, gays and people of color being attacked for seemingly no reason. Rapes and assaults. But a straight white guy, minding his own business? Crazy . . .

John the nurse returned with the promised ice chips and seemed satisfied when Bram ate them easily, reassuring him that his stomach was feeling okay.

"All right," John said. "I'll let you hang on to the cup in that case. Then we'll see about getting something solid into you. How's strawberry jello sound?"

"Terrible."

"You don't like jello?"

"I don't think I've had since I was five."

John chuckled. "We'll see how it goes. Unfortunately, the outgoing phone line in this room is out of service. Don't ask. But is there anyone you'd like us to call? We would have asked you last night but you were in and out of consciousness."

"Uh . . . " Bram hadn't given it any thought. "I can do it. Can you hand me my cellphone?"

"You didn't have one when you were brought in."

Bram frowned, then remembered. "Shit! The bitch that ran me down took it."

"She took your phone?"

"She asked to borrow it. I should have known something was up. Who doesn't have their own phone these days?"

"Okay, don't overexcite yourself. I can bring you a phone. I know the police mentioned they wanted to speak with you a little more later today so you can talk to them about your stolen property."

"They'll be able to trace it or something, right?"

"I'd imagine so. You just relax and have some more ice, okay? Take it slow though. No gobbling. I'll be back in a few minutes with your jello."

John left Bram alone again, with only the sounds of beeping machinery and whatever noise came from the hall through the open doorway. Bram balled his hands into fists, thinking of what had happened to him. The more he thought about it, the more angry he became. For all he knew, he'd never fucking walk again and why? Because he'd rear-ended some bitch who'd slammed on her brakes? He hoped the nurse would bring him a phone soon. He wanted to call his best friend Fulton and let him know what had happened. Maybe start him down the path of a good injury lawyer while Bram was stuck in the hospital. He supposed he should call his parents as well. Maybe a couple other people.

He chewed ice thoughtfully, his fury almost overtaking the pain he was in. For the first time, he thought about his truck, supposing it had been towed. He'd have to ask someone about that. Probably the cops would know and maybe he could talk Fulton into going to get it for him.

Movement in the hall caught his attention. A young woman had paused out there, just beyond the threshold of his room, head bent as she studied the cellphone in her hand.

"Oh, hey," he called. "Excuse me?"

She looked up at him with a questioning expression.

"Do you think I could borrow your phone for a second?"

"Huh?"

"I just need to make a quick phone call. I'd really appreciate it."

"How about fuck you?"

He was taken aback. He stared at her for a moment and she stared back at him. The longer their eye contact continued, the deeper her frown became.

"Use your own fucking phone," she said, finally.

"I don't have one."

"There's one on your bedside table, dumbass."

"They said it's out of—"

"You thought you'd bother a complete stranger instead? I suppose you want me to walk over there and wait on you too, right? Maybe dial the number for you? Don't want to strain your fingers?"

The woman was clearly nuts. "Okay, never mind. Thanks anyway."

"You're lucky I don't throw my phone at your head, asshole." The woman flipped him the bird and disappeared from sight, leaving Bram confused and bristling with anger. What the fuck was that about? Was he on the damn psych ward or something?

He eyed the phone on the table next to his bed with malice.

His headache was getting worse, his ice was melting, and he was beginning to feel more sorry for himself. He suspected shit was going to get a lot worse before it got better.

6

Nicki had stopped by her apartment very quickly after she'd left the store, just long enough to grab some cash and a few changes of clothing. She'd been driving ever since, assuming there would be a warrant out for her arrest. She didn't know very much about the law but obviously cracking your boss upside the head with a heavy bottle was certain to land you in some very hot water. It wasn't like he hadn't had it coming though, embarrassing her the way he did, siding with that asshole. She wondered who Mike would have sided with if the customer had been a woman. In that case, he'd probably have been indifferent, but had she, the cashier, been a dude and the customer a female, then of course, he would have sided with the cashier. She knew how this shit played out. Every. Goddamn. Time. Bros before ho's, after all.

She was reluctant to leave town if for no other reason than the hope that she might just stumble into the asshole customer somewhere, somehow. She'd been fantasizing about that encounter all night.

It was weird. She'd never been violent before but lately . . . lately everything rubbed her the wrong way. Or maybe it was that she was finally seeing things for how they really were. She was seeing *men* for how they really were. Only out for themselves and each other. Sure, they wanted to fuck you—that had never been an issue for her—but now she suspected gay girls were the ones who'd had it right all along. Her friend Marge was a lesbian and Nicki had listened to her complain more than once about how guys, and sometimes girls too, were always fetishizing lesbians and challenging them on how gay they *really* were. Things like, "Yeah, but you'd still fuck Hugh Jackman, right?" Stupid shit like that. Nicki had sympathized. She'd always known men were idiots but more like just dopes. Big, dumb, goofy dogs, but cute sometimes. Nice sometimes too.

Now she saw the truth. Even if they were cute, they were only nice when they wanted something. And what they usually wanted was pussy.

Everything was clear to her now. It was like someone had flipped a switch in her, turning on the lights and waking her up to reality.

She had every right to be pissed off. She—and every other woman on planet Earth—had been pissed *on* for long enough. Nicki was taking a stand, once and for all.

She was driving aimlessly down a rural road when she turned her car around, deciding to head back to town. When she came to a grocery store parking lot, she parked in the most crowded area and went inside, purchasing a pair of cheap scissors. Back in the car, she cut off as much of her hair as she could, stuffing the cuttings in an old fast food bag she'd had stashed between the sheets. Then she added the scissors themselves to the bag and left the car, carrying it with her to the nearest bus stop, where she tossed it in the trash and boarded the next bus for downtown. She decided to play it smart and switched buses more than she needed to, but by early afternoon she was in Marge's neighborhood. They weren't best friends or anything—cops wouldn't think to search for her there—but Nicki thought they were close enough that Marge would let her crash for a while, until she figured out her next move.

Marge lived on the top floor of a three family house and Nicki bounded up the stairs two at a time, anxious to get inside and hopefully get something to drink. She was parched.

When she knocked on Marge's door, it occurred to her that maybe her friend wouldn't be home but at least one of her roommates would be. Nicki had met both of them a couple times and they seemed cool enough. She was surprised though when no one she knew answered the door. Instead, it was an older woman, middle-aged, short, with a wild tangle of graying-brown hair with a single braid amidst the nest, brightly colored beads at the end of it. Brown, smiling eyes gazed at Nicki with interest.

"Can I help you?" the woman asked. Her voice was low and a little on the raspy side.

"Uh . . . yeah. I'm looking for Marge."

"Oh, I'm sorry. She's not home right now."

"Huh." Nicki checked out the woman, who wore one of those blouses Nicki thought of as hippie, old jeans and sandals. Definitely a hippie. "Are you one of her roommates?"

The woman laughed. "I'm her original roommate, sweetie. I'm her mom."

"*Ohhh.* Oh, hi. I'm her friend, Nicki. Any idea when she'll be back?"

The woman glanced over her shoulder at a clock. "Probably not till after five. She's at work."

"Damn." That was bad news. Nicki wasn't sure where else to go.

Marge's mom apparently saw the disappointment on Nicki's face. "You're welcome to wait for her though, if you want. I could use the company." She was still smiling. "It's not often I get to meet many of her friends these days and I was just about to make myself an egg salad sandwich, if you're hungry."

Nicki shifted her weight from one foot to the other, considering. On one hand, there was a lot of hours between now and five, which might be awkward. On the other, she wanted to get out of sight and she *was* pretty hungry. She realized she hadn't eaten anything since the previous afternoon before work.

"Okay," she said, offering her own, however disingenuous, smile.

Marge's mom pulled the door wider, allowing Nicki inside and offered her hand. "I'm Shirley," she said as they shook.

"Nicki."

Shirley closed the door and said, "Oh, Marge has talked about you!"

"Good stuff, I hope."

"Absolutely. So, can I interest you in a sandwich?"

"Yeah, that sounds great. I'm starving."

More smiles. "Follow me."

Shirley was one of the most talkative people Nicki had ever met and over the course of her chatter, Nicki learned that she identified as queer, which surprised her.

"You and Marge are both gay?" Nicki asked, incredulous.

Laughing, Shirley said, "Don't worry. I have a straight daughter too. But, I'm actually . . . bisexual, I suppose. Maybe even pansexual. I think that's what younger folks call it now anyway. Not that I explore those things much anymore. Happily single at the moment."

49

Because she wasn't sure what to say, Nicki nodded and drank from the glass of lemonade Shirley had given her with the sandwich. She hadn't met very many older people who identified as gay . . . or queer . . . and the ones she'd met had all been men.

"You seem mystified," Shirley said. She seemed amused.

"Oh, I, uh . . . no. Just thinking."

"How about you?" Shirley asked.

"I'm not gay," Nicki said, probably too quickly. "I mean, I'm cool with people who are. I kinda wish I was sometimes, to tell you the truth."

"You're not the first woman I've heard say that," Shirley laughed. "But I meant, are you single?"

"Oh! Yeah. Thank fucking god." She grimaced. "Excuse my French."

Shirley began clearing their empty plates from the table. "Bad experiences, I take it?"

Nicki dug gum out of her pocket and tossed a piece in her mouth. "Guys suck."

"Trust me, all people can suck, regardless of sex or gender."

"True," Nicki agreed. "But gay people don't seem as bad."

Shirley's laughter boomed loud at that. "I don't know where you're getting your information on that one, sweetie."

"You don't read the news much, do you?" Nicki

asked.

"As little as possible."

"Then you don't know how bad it's gotten. Men have become monsters. No joke. Always raping, beating, murdering. It's fucking insane."

"I'm sure it's just being reported more, kiddo." Shirley wiped her hands on a dishtowel before returning to the table and sitting across from Nicki.

"I don't think so," Nicki said. "They really have gotten worse. It's like someone gave them permission to just do whatever they want and now their true selves have emerged."

"Wow," Shirley raised her eyebrows. "That's quite a statement."

"They're all happy to let out their inner Mr. Hyde now. And they don't even get punished for it! In fact, they rally around each other when one of them *might* get in trouble. I'm telling you, it's a huge problem now. The government is even involved. Judges, politicians. You name it. It's crazy."

Shirley was nodding and giving Nicki a strange look, like maybe she thought Nicki had recently escaped from the lunatic asylum. Nicki decided to shut up, chewing her gum. Probably no woman Shirley's age would want to hear the truth. Hell, even younger women didn't want to hear it sometimes. But the truth was in everyone's pockets. All they had to do was look at their phones and they'd see it with their own eyes. Finally, she asked Shirley, "You want some gum?"

"No, thank you," Shirley said. "Would you like more lemonade?"

"Okay."

Shirley rose and went to the refrigerator, where she paused, then turned to face Nicki again. "You know what? I think I might want something stronger."

"Sounds good," Nicki said.

"Marge only ever has beer, so you can have beer if you want. I'm more of a Wild Turkey gal myself and you're also welcome to join me in a glass of that."

Nicki thought about it. "Wild Turkey would be great."

7

The ER doctor told Mark he was lucky to be alive as he was stitching him up. If his wife had used a larger pair of scissors—or anything else, really—he most certainly wouldn't be.

Mark didn't feel particularly lucky. In fact, he felt decidedly *unlucky* as he lay in his hospital bed, in pain, but probably going to be released soon. It had been a long, exhausting night but apparently he was in good enough shape to go home. No fever had sprung up and though he felt crushed, he didn't appear to have suffered a mental breakdown over the domestic violence that had befallen him.

He wasn't sure he agreed with that one but he now had a new piece of paper in his wallet, listing several therapists who dealt with this kind of thing listed on it. He'd never seen a therapist before and the idea made him nervous. He figured he'd see how it went before making a decision on that front. More pressing in his mind was the location of his wife and why she'd gone completely insane so abruptly. He debated on calling the kids but wasn't sure how he'd tell them what had happened, particularly the part where no one seemed to know where Patti was at the moment. He supposed it was possible she was with one of them, but he doubted it. Certainly, they would have called if that had been the case. They would want answers, of course. Maybe even blame him for the attack, depending on what she told them.

Mark wondered if, in fact, it *had* been his fault. Some of what she'd said had been true. Like the things about their sex life.

A nurse walked into the room, disrupting his thoughts. She was short and plump, middle-aged, and had the air of someone who'd been doing the job for long enough to be burned out on it.

"How are you feeling, Mr. Gray?"

He tried to smile. "Like I've been stabbed a dozen times and have about forty stitches in my torso. Not to mention the broken nose."

The nurse didn't return the smile, just stared at him, hand on hip. "Well, I think you'll live."

That struck him as a rather cold thing to say and his brow furrowed as he considered a reply but she didn't give him an opportunity to form one.

"You can start getting dressed," she said. "Do

you have someone who can drive you home?"

"No," he said. "I guess I could call someone."

"Then you want to do that."

He thought about it, unable to think of anyone he'd want knowing about this, for lack of a better term, domestic dispute.

"Or we can call you a cab."

"That might be better."

She pulled a plastic bag from inside the closet and tossed it onto his lap. "All your belongings are in here. I'll be back with your paperwork and prescriptions." She exited the room without waiting for a response, leaving Mark to ponder how someone could have such a terrible bedside manner.

He checked the contents of the bag, which only included the boxers he'd been wearing when he'd been admitted, plus his wallet and phone. Assuming the hospital would at least give him scrubs and slippers to wear, he didn't understand why they weren't in the bag to begin with. Probably the nurse would bring them when she returned with the other things.

Getting out of the bed was pure agony and he wondered how on earth they could be releasing him less than 24 hours after he'd been stabbed multiple times. He understood the wounds were shallow, but still, it seemed odd. He shrugged off the hospital gown and leaned on the bed, struggling into the boxers slowly, one foot at a time. Bending over to pull them up, he soon discovered, was next to impossible.

He'd never been in such pain before. The entire process, pulling the underwear all the way up, took him nearly five minutes.

Sweat ran down his forehead and sides in rivulets, stinging his eyes and dampening the waist band of the boxers. His breathing became panting and his face scrunched into a tortured countenance. When he finally looked up, he saw the nurse standing in the hallway, watching him with, it seemed to him, amusement.

"Enjoying the show?" he snapped. "What's wrong with you? Aren't you supposed to help me?"

"You have to do things on your own, Mr. Gray," she said, entering the room. She held a small pharmaceutical bag in one hand, a clipboard in the other, maroon scrubs thrown over one shoulder. "I'm going to ask you to put these on and then we're going to take a walk around the floor. How's that sound?"

"Do I have a choice?" Mark was rarely ever so surly, but now he was just pissed off.

"No," the nurse said, tossing the meds bag on the bed followed by the scrubs. "Get dressed."

It was the last straw.

"What in the hell is wrong with you?" Mark demanded. "Can't you see I'm in pain? Aren't you supposed to have at least a modicum of sympathy in your line of work?"

She took a couple steps towards him. "You're not in even half the pain a lot of people here are. Do you understand the world doesn't revolve around you? I goddamn doubt it. People here are dying and boohoo, you got poked a few times. Poor baby. I just wonder what you did to provoke her and don't even think about telling me it was nothing because I know better. Most women know better. The only ones stupid enough to believe your dumb sob story are other idiots with fleshy chads hanging between their legs and I doubt even they believe it. Not really. They just feel for you because, oh my god, a woman had the audacity to stand up for herself for probably the first time in her life. She decided she was done with your pathetic bullshit and gave it right back to you. Didn't she? Isn't that what happened, Mark? And now, *she'll* be the one punished, just like it always happens. Can't have a woman stand up for herself, can you? Oh, no, God forbid! She needs to be punished and punished good! Made an example of, isn't that right, Mr. Gray? So any woman watching will know she better sit down and shut up. She better know her goddamn place or else! Do exactly as she's told or there'll be hell to pay, right? *Right?"*

Mark could only stare. He was stunned into silence, watching as this woman's face darkened and morphed into blind rage. Her eyes seethed with pure hatred and he was positive she would attack him, lash out in the same way Patti had done. Swallowing the lump that had formed in his throat, Mark took a deep breath and then began shouting for help.

The nurse's response was to take the final step towards him and stab a thumb into a puncture wound by his left nipple. He screamed in pain and terror as she bent over, putting her face right in his. "You need to calm the fuck down, Mr. Gray," she hissed quietly. Then louder, "Oops. What happened there, honey? Pulled a stitch, did you? I'll fix that right up for you."

"*Help!*" Mark shrieked. "*Jesus, god, help me! She's insane!*" He attempted to turn his body from her, shielding his chest with his arms, feeling fresh blood trickling. "*Get away from me!*"

"Calm down, Mr. Gray," the nurse said, her voice almost soothing.

"Everything okay in here?"

Mark looked over the psychotic nurse's shoulder and saw another nurse in the doorway. Younger, prettier, probably Latino or maybe Greek. Her expression showed pure boredom.

"Help me!" Mark cried. "This woman assaulted me!"

The first nurse laughed heartily. "We have a live one here, Marie."

Completely ignoring Mark, Marie asked the older nurse, "You okay?"

"Oh, yeah. Totally under control." She looked down at Mark. "He's just got some pain going on but he'll be okay as long as he sits still while I help him get dressed. Already popped a stitch with all his flailing around." She chuckled. "Naturally, he thinks that's my fault."

"Don't listen to her," Mark said, barely able to catch his breath. "She did this to me!" He pointed to his newly bleeding chest wound. "She did it on purpose!"

Marie tilted her head, scowling slightly, her eyes on his and there was a moment when he thought they made a silent connection, that she believed him. But then she looked at the older nurse, Mildred, according to her nametag, and gave her a sympathetic half smile. "They might have space on 3 North."

"That's not a bad idea," Mildred said, eyeing Mark.

"What's that?" he asked, uncomfortable with how high his voice was getting. "What is that?"

Shaking her head, Marie walked off, leaving him alone with the evil nurse once more. She smiled down at him and said, "Psych ward."

8

Much to their surprise and delight, like the restaurant, the used book store was also strangely empty. Ariana and Jaclyn separated soon after entering, as they usually did. Jaclyn was more into fantasy and science fiction, so she headed for that part of the store, whereas Ariana always wanted to check out the LGBTQ section first before making her way over to the horror shelves.

It was here, while she perused the hardcovers shelves, that she heard yet another argument between a man and a woman. Curious, she put the book she'd been looking at back where she'd found it and casually walked in the direction of the voices, taking care to not look directly at the quarreling pair. Instead, she focused on what turned out to be the self-help section.

"I honestly don't give a shit," the woman said. "You left early yesterday, you're not doing it again today." Mid-twenties, average height and build, pretty red hair.

"But my aunt is really sick," the guy replied. He was tall and thin, mussed black hair falling over his forehead as he pushed black-framed glasses up his nose. "She might die."

"That's what you said yesterday."

"So? It's true."

"You think just because you come in every day, you're not going to get reprimanded for taking off early? That's not how this works, Joseph."

The woman's voice was rising, both in pitch and volume.

"That's not . . . " He stammered. "I just got the call from my mother, Gayle. I have to go."

"For your dying aunt, who you're *so* close to, right? The one you've literally *never* mentioned before this week?"

Joseph shoved his glasses up again and fidgeted with a class ring on his finger. He said nothing, but looked pathetic.

"If you want to keep lying to me, feel free," Gayle told him. "But, I'm telling you right now, you walk out that door today and you're fired."

"What? You can't fire me for that!"

"Watch me," Gayle snapped, turning her back on his and starting to walk away.

"Please!" Joseph followed, reaching out to touch her shoulder.

Ariana was stunned when Gayle whirled around, grabbed the nearest hardcover book within her reach and clubbed Joseph across the head with it. His glasses went flying as he staggered sideways with a grunt. If not for the bookshelf to his right, he would have toppled to the floor.

"Hey!" Ariana shouted, stepping forward, arms outstretched to block any further attacks. "Are you out of your mind, lady? You just assaulted this guy!"

Gayle did her best to dance around Ariana, trying to whack Joseph again. He stood dazed, one hand pressed to the side of his head.

"Stop!" Ariana cried, doing her best to block access to the man without touching the woman.

"What the hell is going on?" Jaclyn said, coming up behind both Joseph and Ariana.

"This chick is nuts," Ariana said, genuinely angry. Over her shoulder, she told Joseph, "I'll be your witness if you want to press charges."

"Oh, mind your own goddamn business," Gayle said, her fury clearly growing. "Find another dick to suck because he won't be interested. Isn't that right, Joseph?"

More people were gathering round, drawn by the commotion, three women and one elderly man. They stood back, though Ariana noted one of the women recording everyone with her cellphone.

Gayle went on, spittle flying from her lips. "Joseph here thinks the misogynist politicians are doing a *great* job, don't you, Joseph? He doesn't see any problem with their behavior and even likes their tweets!"

The woman recording the incident gasped while the other two women made sounds of disgust.

"So what?" the elderly man croaked. He was rail-thin, holding a Hemingway paperback in his gnarled hand. "Everyone is entitled to his own opinion."

Gayle sneered at the man. "Oh, another one, ladies. What a surprise."

The women stepped away from the man as though he might be carrying a contagion of some kind, noses crinkled and eyes narrowed.

Even Ariana glanced again at Joseph, momentarily seeing something akin to a slug, maybe. Perhaps a roach. Then she shook the feeling off and saw only a young man who looked excessively nervous, still pressing a hand to the side of his head.

The elderly man took a step forward and shook a bony finger at Gayle. "Shame on you!"

"Shame *this!*" Gayle grabbed both of her breasts in her hands and shook them vigorously at the man.

Startled, Ariana had to stifle a laugh but the amusement she felt didn't last long.

The old man's watery blue eyes widened considerably and when he spoke, it was barely above a whisper. "You're just a punk! I hope your daddy paddles you good and hard!"

Jaclyn balked. "Wow."

Gayle stunned everyone by grabbing yet another hardback book off the shelf and whipped it at the old man. The loft was all wrong though and it fell harmlessly at his feet as she bellowed, "My daddy's been dead for over a decade, you shriveled old cocksucker!"

"Your husband then!" the elderly man hollered right back and began walking away. "I'm reporting you to the authorities!"

"My *husband*!" Gayle shrieked. "You're saying my *husband* should beat *me*?"

"Yes! Someone should!"

Gayle charged after him and Ariana was no longer worried about Joseph. "Oh, shit."

Shoving the old man to the floor, Gayle proceeded to begin kicking him. Hard.

Ariana hurried over, unable to believe what was happening. "Call the police!" she shouted as she tried to restrain Gayle, catching an elbow to the face. Knocked off balance, she glanced back at Jaclyn, who stood with her mouth hanging open. "Jac! Call the fucking cops!"

"I don't have my phone!"

Fuck.

The elderly man fought back but he was losing and started hissing obscenities, using probably every derogatory term for female he'd ever heard in his life.

The woman who'd been recording the whole thing looked around. "What did he just say?"

Ariana had roughly half a second to see where this was headed. She looked past the advancing women to Jaclyn. Their eyes met. Everything seemed to be happening in slow motion. Jaclyn turned to look back at Joseph, who was already on the move, but heading away from everyone else, towards the front of the store. Hopefully to call 911.

Stretching out her arms, Ariana braced for impact as the other three woman charged forth, clearly more than willing to mow her down in their desire to get to the old man. One of the women spit directly at her, snarling the word *traitor* before throwing a fist. The blow connected with Ariana's right eye and down she went, tripping over both Gayle and the old man, landing hard enough to knock the wind out of her.

Jaclyn shouted, launching herself at Ariana's attacker.

Dazed, the words that came to Ariana's mind were *girl fight*.

The inside of the bookstore became an all out brawl, Jaclyn repeatedly belting the woman, who had turned away, covering her head with her arms while Jac beat on her back and sides, swearing. The other two women continued to kick the old man who'd finally stopped his bellowing.

Ariana got to her feet and grabbed the arm of one of the women, yanking her back, shouting "Stop!"

The old man grunted as he was kicked in the stomach and chest.

"I called the cops," Joseph shouted.

The woman Ariana had been attempting to restrain pulled herself free and went for Joseph instead, grabbing him around the neck. Suddenly, all three of the women were focused on the younger man, abandoning their other opponents.

Joseph ran away, the women in pursuit. Ariana stooped to help the old man up and Jaclyn came to join her. They both grabbed him beneath his arms and assisted him to his feet. His lips were split, blood dripping from his chin, and a knot was already forming on his forehead. Ariana noted he was now toothless, the dentures kicked clean out of his mouth.

"We need to get out of here," Jaclyn said. She was already developing a shiner and Ariana had to wonder if she too had any battle wounds.

From another part of the store, Joseph began to scream.

"Oh, my god," Ariana said, her stomach suddenly rolling. "Are they killing him?"

"We need to *go*," Jaclyn insisted.

"But the cops . . . "

"It'll probably take them ten minutes to get here."

Between them, the old man began to weep.

"*Fuck!*" Ariana didn't know what to do. Leaving the scene didn't seem like a good idea but staying here . . . she didn't want to still be around when they were finished with Joseph. "Ok, let's go."

The hurried to the exit, the old man propped between them. As the left, two more women entered. "Don't go in there," Ariana told them. "Just call 911."

The warning garnered her puzzled glances and was promptly ignored. If anything, the women seemed more anxious to get inside.

They crossed the parking lot, just short of running. To their amazement, more people were shouting outside. Another physical altercation was about to begin.

9

Bram wanted out of this damn hospital. He didn't care if he had a concussion.

"Nurse!" he shouted. *"Nurse!"*

He knew he had a button to push in the event he needed assistance, but, really, fuck that. It sounded like someone was having a fist fight in the hallway though, so he doubted anyone would be by to attend to him anyway. But it still didn't stop him from trying.

"Nurse! John!"

Much to his surprise, John came in, eyebrows raised in question, though he stopped just past the threshold of the door. "What do you need, Bram?" He was somewhat out of breath.

"I want out of here. Tell the doctor."

"That's it?"

His response annoyed Bram. "What do you mean, *that's it*? I want out! Some bitch just threatened to throw a phone at my head and now it sounds like someone—probably *her*—is whaling on some other poor bastard."

John looked over his shoulder, back into the hall. When he turned back to Bram, he said, "We have a situation, but it's being controlled."

"It doesn't sound like it's being controlled."

"Do you need something immediately, Bram?"

"I just told you what I need. I want to talk to the doctor."

Down the hall, a man began to screech in what sounded like real pain and John ran out of Bram's room.

"Son of a bitch!" Bram cursed. He'd never felt so helpless in his life. Trapped in this damn bed with a busted leg and maybe a busted head, though he was beginning to doubt the latter. He mostly felt okay. Maybe it was the meds making him feel okay, but he hoped not.

He sat there stewing for a minute or so, listening to the commotion as his agitation receded. Two guys raced by his room, orderlies by the looks of them, and after that the hospital got fairly quiet. Eventually, a couple cops walked by and he eagerly awaited seeing the woman who had threatened him carted off, but instead, he began to doze off out of boredom.

"Bram?"

Startled, he opened his eyes to see not John but a woman in a lab coat. A doctor, thank fucking god. Doctor Jeanine Walker.

She asked all the typical questions about pain levels and how he felt in general and he answered them dutifully until he couldn't stand it anymore and blurted, "I want to go home."

Much to his surprise, after a quick scan of his chart, she told him they could get started on his release and would send someone in with a wheelchair.

He sighed. "Thank you!"

"We just have to get you some paperwork and see how you do on the crutches."

"The crutches?"

"Yeah, don't worry about it. You'll be fine but we're gonna have a physical therapist help you out with that first."

"I think I can figure out crutches on my own." He chuckled without humor. "I definitely don't need anyone to show me anything like that."

"It's procedure," Dr. Walker told him.

"But . . . " He closed his eyes and rubbed his forehead with the tips of his fingers. "Okay, fine. How long will that take?"

She checked her watch, clicking the pen in her free hand. "Hmm. Not sure if she'll be able to get to you today."

"*What?* I just got finished telling you I want out of here!"

"Calm down, Bram. We'll do everything we can to make that happen, okay? We just need—"

"Is this an insurance scam or something?" he demanded. "It's ridiculous! You can't keep me here against my will!"

"We need to make sure it's safe to release you. We could be held liable if we let you go home and you got hurt as a result of that."

"I'll sign something, okay? Anything you want me to sign. I won't sue, I promise. And besides, nothing bad will even happen."

They went back and forth for several minutes, Bram becoming increasingly upset until finally he snapped and said he'd sue if they *didn't* release him, which caused her to leave the room, saying she'd be back when he had calmed down. The whole situation was bullshit and he'd had enough.

Tossing back the sheet and blanket covering him, he was determined to get out of the bed and get the fuck out of this place. His leg was casted from his toes to the middle of his thigh. The skin above the cast was a sunset of bruises, surprising him. The instant he tried to move the leg, pain shot through it and he cried out, stilling himself immediately. He cursed and then cursed again.

A nurse who wasn't John entered the room, took one look at him and said, "You don't want to do that."

He regarded her through squinted eyes, his hands balled into fists.

The woman came to the side of the bed and pulled the covers up over him again. "I have some pain meds for you," she said.

There was something about her that seemed robotic. Her face was expressionless, her voice flat. It made Bram uncomfortable.

"I have some meds for you." She showed him a tiny paper cup. "Open up."

"What is it?"

"Something for the pain. It'll help you relax."

Bram frowned.

She shook the cup, the pills rattling together. "Open."

He hesitated. "Where is the physical therapist?"

"I'll have to get back to you on that."

She stared at him and he stared back. He noticed her eyes were very green.

"Open," she said.

He did as he was told and she plopped the pills into his mouth, handing him the plastic bottle of water. He sipped and swallowed.

"Good boy," she said, though her expression didn't change and, really, he hadn't expected it to.

There was something about her that made him nervous. Beyond nervous, even. A sense that she could—and maybe *would*—be dangerous for him if he pissed her off. Despite the fact she hadn't raised her voice, hadn't said anything at all to give him the impression he had and yet, there it was. And now he was thinking about it, the doctor had had the same air about her. A cold, distant vibe which told him not to press his luck with them. With the nurse, it was stronger, as though she would have far less patience than the doctor had.

"Sit tight," she said. "I'll check back with you in a little while."

He nodded, silent, and watched her go. He wanted to get out of here now more than ever but he couldn't shake the anxious feeling. Wondering where John had gone, he lay back on his pillows and stared up at the blank television mounted on the wall. He glanced around for the remote control that should have been nearby but he didn't see it. So now he was stuck without a phone and without a TV. Surely the other guys at work had noticed his absence. Maybe someone would think to call around to hospitals. Maybe even the police. They were sure to have a record of the accident and the batshit bitch who'd put him in here. His buddy Fulton would have tried calling him by now and would almost certainly try again before nightfall.

For now, though, he supposed he was stuck with naval gazing, at least until the physical therapist showed up.

10

By the time Marge got home from work, Nicki and Shirley were pretty trashed and having the time of their lives. Nicki, even though it had only been a few hours, absolutely adored Shirley and had told her several times over how much she wished Shirley were *her* mom.

Shirley was tickled, laughing uproariously every time Nicki said it.

They sat together slouched on the couch, feet kicked up on the coffee table, clicking their glasses together every few minutes, sometimes sloshing booze onto their own bellies.

Marge came in a little after 5 pm, a long bag slung over her shoulder, her thick red hair curling around her tired but pretty face. She was surprised to see Nicki.

"Hey!"

"Hey, yourself," Nicki said, greeting her friend by waving the glass at her.

Shirley jumped up off the couch and ran to Marge, planting a sloppy kiss on her cheek. "We missed you!"

Dropping her bag onto an armchair, Marge glanced between the two of them, looking somewhat amused. "Hitting the bottle, are we?"

"No time like the present," Nicki said, smiling. She knew she was drunk, but not *that* drunk. Trashed, yes, but she wasn't going to puke or anything. The room wasn't spinning. She was simply having a good time. She was happy and couldn't remember the last time she'd felt anything close to that. "Join us."

"Yeah, baby, join us!" Shirley kissed her daughter's cheek again, wrapping an arm around her neck and nearly pulling her off balance.

"First, I want to eat something," Marge said, untangling herself from her mother.

"I'll make you something," Shirley volunteered. "What would you like?"

"I was thinking Caesar salad."

"I already made chicken! You need your protein." Shirley trotted happily off to the kitchen.

Marge plopped herself down onto the armchair, tossing her bag on the floor.

"Your mom is awesome," Nicki said, reaching over to slap her friend's knee.

"She's pretty cool, yeah."

"And she's gay too! Just like you! How fucking awesome is that?"

Lifting an eyebrow, Marge said, "She told you she's gay?"

"Yeah, is she not?"

"No, I think she is. She just never uses that word."

"Oh, yeah. I think she said bi."

Marge laughed. "Exactly. Never mind that she hasn't had a boyfriend since I was born."

"Still technically bi," Shirley called from the kitchen.

Nicki and Marge exchanged *whoops* looks before Marge called back, "Yeah, whatever you say, Mom."

"Anyway," Nicki said. "It's cool that you have something to bond over like that?"

Marge made a face. "Do you and your mom bond over being straight?"

Nicki knew Marge was somewhat offended and quickly said, "No, we don't bond over anything." There was an awkward pause, then she said, "So . . . how's work?"

"It's a thrift store. Same shit every day." She stood up. "I'm gonna grab a beer, okay?"

"No Wild Turkey for you?"

"Nah. Beer is good. Be right back."

After Marge left the room, Nicki drained her glass and sucked on an ice cube. She eyed the bottle of booze on the table, debating on a refill then decided to check her phone instead. She half expected to find an email from her boss telling her she was fired but there was nothing. She wondered again if he might be dead. She didn't think she'd hit him *that* hard but maybe he had a soft skull or something.

She was just about to check the news when Marge came back, beer in hand, flopping herself back into the chair. "Mom wants to know if you want any salad."

"No, thanks."

"No, thanks!" Marge shouted.

Marge took a slug of her beer then asked, "How's your job going? Still at the drug store?"

"As far as I know," Nicki said. "But maybe not."

"What does that mean?"

Nicki thought about it for a second but decided she wasn't drunk enough to spill the beans on herself. That would probably be a super stupid move. "You know. I'm just fed up with it. My boss is a dick."

"Every boss is a dick."

"True. The customers suck too."

"All customers suck."

"Agreed." Nicki decided she'd have another drink after all and helped herself. She didn't think Shirley would mind. She was replacing the bottle's cap when Shirley returned, with a big plastic bowl of salad for Marge.

"Awesome," Marge said, accepting it. "Thanks, Mom."

Shirley took her place beside Nicki on the couch once more. "Christian and Beth wanted me to tell you they were going up north, by the way."

Christian and Beth were Marge's roommates.

"What for?" Marge asked around a mouthful of lettuce.

"I didn't ask." Shirley shrugged. "Assumed they were going up to see Beth's family."

"Probably," Marge agreed. "Weird to go during the week though. I hope nothing bad happened."

"I didn't get that impression at all."

Nicki had only met the roommates a couple times so she kept her mouth shut and drank her Turkey. Her buzz was growing but she was no longer feeling as happy. She shouldn't have checked her phone. Now she was too busy thinking about her asshole boss and that had killed her buzz. In a way, she was hoping she *had* killed him. Would serve him right, after the way he'd handled the situation with that fuckhead customer. She wondered what the prison sentence would be for murder as opposed to attempted murder, which she assumed is what they would charge her with, even though she hadn't been thinking about either thing. Not that she remembered anyway. If anything, in her mind, she should maybe just get assault. There was the whole *deadly weapon* part of it though. She was sure they'd throw that one in her face.

"Earth to Nicki."

She looked up to see Shirley laughing at her, waving the bottle playfully.

"Want another?"

Nicki thought about it.

"She has to drive, Mom," Marge said.

"Oh, she's past driving," Shirley said. "She can crash on the couch."

"*You're* sleeping on the couch."

"No, Beth said I could have their room, if I wanted it and you can be damn sure I do."

"Oh. Well, in that case, Nicki, you're welcomed to stay."

"She's staying. No drinking and driving. Doctor Mom says so." Shirley laughed again, clearly intoxicated. Her cheeks had gone an impossible shade of red.

"Okay," Nicki said. "I'll crash here *and* have another drink."

"That's the spirit!" Shirley practically shouted. "Party hardy!"

Nicki laughed but Marge let out a little groan. "It's kind of embarrassing when you say that, Mom."

"What?" Shirley asked. "Party hardy?"

"Yes."

"I've been saying it for decades."

"I *know*."

When the laughter had died down a little, Nicki blurted out, "I may have killed my boss today."

The other two women stopped laughing abruptly, stared at her, then began to laugh even harder.

Nicki smiled over the rim of her glass, starting to feel happy again.

11

3 North.

Third floor, north wing.

How Mark had ended up here, he had no idea. True, he'd begun screaming his balls off after that crazy nurse had threatened him, after she'd assaulted him, but he knew anyone in the same position would have done the exact same thing. Probably with the same result, he assumed. So, looking at it that way, he supposed he did know how he'd gotten here.

They'd dressed him in maroon scrubs and put him in a smaller part of the psych ward, what was, he learned, known as 'the dark half.' It was where the potentially dangerous people were placed, the real psychos. That was the impression he'd received anyway. He'd had to promise to behave himself on the trip over, lest they strap him to a gurney and sedate him.

He'd made the promise and kept to his word. Like a good little boy, he thought now, resentfully, as he sat in what passed as a common room, which was no more than a small room with a television, one reclining chair and a love seat, both of which had seen better days.

Mark was on the love seat while another guy sprawled spread-eagle in the recliner, face pointed towards a window but just staring off into space. The TV was on and Mark watched it absently, retaining none of what was happening on the screen. His mind was elsewhere.

To the left was a desk where a nurse stood, tapping away on a computer keyboard. Mark had already seen that another monitor was reserved for viewing the interior of the private rooms, which were equipped with security cameras mounted high on the walls. The staff kept a close eye on the patients, presumably to be sure no one was hurting themselves or anyone else.

The attending nurse left her work station briefly and returned with meds. She stood in front of the television, completely blocking it from Mark's view, and said, "Time for your medication, Russell."

For a second, Mark assumed she was calling him by the wrong name until he realized she was speaking to the guy in the recliner. Russell continued to gaze out the window until she said his name again, at which point he informed her that he wouldn't be taking his meds today.

"Come on, Russell," she said. "Let's not do this again."

Finally, Russell looked at the nurse. "I'm an American citizen. You can't make me do shit."

"I'm not going to ask you again," the nurse said.

"I don't care. You can't force me. I have civil rights."

"Do you want me to call security?"

"Whatever. Do what you have to do."

Without another word, the woman walked back to her work station and picked up the phone. Russell went back to looking out the window and Mark went back to pretending to watch television. The TV was tuned to a gardening program and Mark supposed if he wanted to learn about growing onions in his home garden (which he didn't have) it would have been interesting viewing.

A few minutes later, uniformed security guards showed up. Two men, looking either jaded or entertained, it was difficult to tell which.

"Okay, Russell," the nurse said.

Russell didn't move.

Up until this point, the nurse seemed completely unaware of Mark's presence but then she asked him to go to his room. He complied without question. As he was walking towards it, down a relatively short hallway, the shouting began behind him.

He didn't look back.

In his room, he lay on his bed and briefly put his hands behind his head, until he felt the pain of his puncture wounds, at which point he readjusted with his arms at his sides. He tried to ignore the commotion happening in the common room, even as the shouter grew louder and more frantic.

Poor Russell.

Mark had to wonder if that guy was also in here due to, essentially, women in power and their angriness. Their spite. Their jealousy and dissatisfaction with their own stations in life.

He glanced up at the camera mounted in the corner near the ceiling and offered up his middle finger to it, knowing full well that the nurse was otherwise occupied. He wished he had the balls of Russell out there, who was having meds shoved down his throat by a stranger while being held down by two guys, each twice his size. Russell was doomed. But Mark was going to get out of here as soon as he fucking could. If he had to play possum to do it, then that's what he'd do. Not make waves.

When the shouting died down, he got up again, walking to the common room in his bare feet, the stiff scrubs rustling and scratching against his skin.

Russell was gone, probably doped up and sleeping in his room, but another guy, just a kid of twenty or so, was seated at the table by the nursing station eating sweetened peaches out of a plastic cup, with a plastic spoon.

Mark nodded at the kid when he looked up but the kid didn't nod back. Then Mark returned to his previous spot on the loveseat. The TV was still on, playing one of those home improvement shows, yet another thing he couldn't have cared less about.

He zoned out, lost in thought and didn't break the surface again until he noticed the staff bring in a new person. He barely glanced up, uninterested, but when he did, he did a double take.

So did she.

His heart screamed in his chest as Patti stared at him, recognition blooming in her face but even more than that: pure hatred was there as well.

Leaping to his feet, Mark shouted, "Patti!"

Before anyone knew what was happening, she was charging him, arms flailing, hands turned into claws.

She leapt across the room like an animal, screeching, an attacking primate, teeth gnashing. She reached him with a flying tackle that would have impressed any football fan and he toppled backwards with her on top of him, scratching, thrashing, punching, even biting.

Mark screamed in pain and terror. Stitches popped in his belly but he barely noticed. His wife was trying her best to scrape out his eyes and tear out his throat. It seemed like an eternity before anyone helped him and then, it wasn't the staff, but the sullen young man who hadn't wanted to acknowledge even a minor greeting.

The kid got Patti off Mark, wrestling her away and getting his own talon scrape across the cheek for his trouble. Mark scrambled to his feet, one hand on his bleeding stomach, as he tried to back away, finding he didn't have much space to back away into. He collided with the wall and the window far too soon for his liking.

Then the staff was there, pulling Patti away, dragging her off down the hall as she spat and swore and struggled. The nurse who had called security earlier came over to find out what had happened. Mark had no idea where she'd been before he'd been attacked but at least she was there now.

"You have to let me out of here," Mark cried. "She wants to kill me!"

The woman lifted his shirt and examined the freshly opened wounds. "We're gonna have to restitch those."

Mark brushed her hands away. "Listen to me! I can't be in here with her! She's the woman who did this to me!"

Her face darkening, the nurse said, "I don't need to be spoken to like that, Mark."

He looked over her shoulder at the kid who'd pulled Patti off him. The young man shrugged, holding a hand to his scratched cheek. Then he shuffled off down the hall, as though he didn't have a care in the world.

"I'm sorry," Mark said slowly, trying to catch his breath. "But you don't understand. That woman is my wife and she tried to kill me."

The nurse looked skeptical. "Is that right?"

"Yes!"

Mark was stunned dumb when she spoke next, asking him, "What did you do to provoke her?"

12

Ariana and Jaclyn learned the old man's name was William once he was safely in the passenger seat of Ariana's hatchback. Jac was in the rear, poking her head out between the front seats. It stuck Ariana as odd they couldn't yet hear sirens, near or far, and she said as much.

Jaclyn said, "Cops always take their damn time. Probably stuffing their faces with doughnuts."

"Wow," Ariana said. "Didn't know you weren't a fan."

"Guess it's never come up, huh?"

"Guess not."

William groaned, holding his side. Ariana suspected he probably had a cracked rib or two but she kept that to herself. The rest of him didn't look too great either. He was holding a napkin up to his bleeding lip with his other hand and his face was swollen and bruising in multiple places. Both she and Jaclyn had also sustained injuries, but nothing too serious, thank god. Nothing an icepack and a couple aspirin wouldn't take care of.

"I can't believe I got jumped by a bunch of *women*," William said. "I'll never live it down. The fellas at the Knights of Columbus will laugh me out of town."

Ariana and Jaclyn exchanged looks via the rear-view mirror but said nothing.

"I swore my whole life I'd never hit a woman," William continued. "But I swear, if I ever see those lunatics again I will drop them like flies! That was nothing but typical feminist bullies. That's what that was."

"Really?" Jaclyn said. "That's what that was?"

"Jac." Ariana said and they made eye contact again. Ari shook her head as subtly as she could and Jaclyn made the universal *my lips are zipped* motion.

"Yes, that's what that was!" William nearly shouted, then winced. More quietly, he asked, "What would you call it?"

"Definitely feminist bullies," Ariana said, keeping her eyes on the road.

"See?" William attempted to turn in his seat to look at Jaclyn but whimpered and thought better of it. "That's what I'm saying."

They drove the rest of the way in silence, but for the occasional moans from William, and when they arrived at the hospital, Ariana and Jaclyn once again propped William up between them and assisted him into the ER, which was bustling. There was a long line at the desk, people with varying degrees of injuries, from broken bones to split heads holding bloody towels to their gaping wounds. Nothing *too* urgent but certainly concerning.

The women waited in line with William until twenty minutes had passed and he insisted they leave him. They argued and eventually the three reached a compromise: he could stand in line on his own but they would stay for him in the waiting area. It didn't seem likely he would be admitted, but, given his age, they couldn't be sure.

Finding seats was a challenge. They ended up having to lean on a wall for quite some time. It was astounding how crowded the ER was. Many of the injured people were men, though there were a couple women and at least four boys.

Ariana found the whole thing to be quite surreal, like a Twilight Zone episode. Even as they waited, observing their surroundings, a fight broke out between a man and one of the few women.

They saw the whole thing unfold in real time.

The woman, probably in her thirties, had been staring at her phone, thumbing through it with one hand while cradling the other in her lap. She'd sustained some sort of hand injury, as the favored one was wrapped with gauze, spots of blood visible.

90

The man seated beside her had blood stained tissue paper plugging his nostrils and two impressive shiners around both eyes. He shifted in his seat, his elbow bumping the arm of the woman beside him.

She looked up from her phone, glaring. "Excuse me!"

"Sorry," he said, through his stuffed nose, then coughed.

"Oh my god!" she said, sounding disgusted. "I can't believe you have the audacity first to decide the arm of my chair is also yours but then you cough right in my face?"

"Sorry," he said again. He was beginning to look perturbed.

"Oh, great," the woman continued. "Now I have to deal with your sarcasm too? Who the fuck do you think you are?"

"I wasn't being sarcastic."

"And there it is again! Sarcasm about your sarcasm. I know men are used to being able to gaslight any women they ever come in contact with, but do I look like a goddamn idiot to you? You know what? Never mind! Don't answer that because you wouldn't be honest anyway."

Clearly out of patience and no longer finding any semblance of politeness in him, he said, "Why don't you just shut up? You're making a scene for no reason."

This, Ariana knew, was the wrong thing to say

and she, along with several other people within ear-shot, winced.

"Don't you fucking tell me to shut up," the woman shouted, getting to her feet, her phone forgotten. "Who the hell do you think you are? Telling a woman to shut up! I don't know what planet you come from, but on *this* one, with this woman? Nobody talks to *me* that way so take your swinging gorilla dick and try shoving that shit down someone else's throat!"

Now most of the people in the waiting area were paying attention, though some of them tried not to stare directly.

"Lady, I don't know what your problem is. Is it that time of the month? Huh? Is that it? Or you just haven't gotten laid in a decade?" The guy was going on a rant now, also getting to his feet. The two of them stood toe to toe, though the man towered over the woman by at least a full foot. "Is that how you hurt your wrist? Flicking it too hard?"

"I'll flick *you* too hard, you stupid son of a bitch!"

"Yeah, how about you flick this?" The guy grabbed his crotch and shook it at her. "Probably be the first time you ever touched one though, huh? You're one of those feminazi liberal dykes, aren't you? Too fucking ugly to get a guy."

Ariana could feel her temperature rising and one glance at Jac told her that she, too, had heard just about enough from this jackass. At first, she had felt a little bad for the guy, but, sure enough, he was showing his true colors.

"You guys are all broken records," the woman said. "It's no wonder someone punched you in the face. If you were my man, I'd clock you with a god-damn frying pan."

The woman seemed to be calming down, oddly enough. She seemed almost amused now.

"If I was your man, I'd fucking *let* you!"

A bunch of the surrounding men began to snicker, which made Ariana increasingly uncomfortable.

Sitting down once more, the woman waved a dismissive hand at the man. As far as she was concerned, she was done with him.

But he didn't feel the same. The chuckling audience was all the encouragement he needed to keep going. Looking around with a smirk, he swung his arm a little, as though he were a boxer playing tough guy in a ring. "You're probably an SJW."

The woman made a show of rolling her eyes, but said nothing and went back to looking at her phone. Or at least pretending to.

Unsatisfied with this response, he ventured on. "Let me guess. You think if a guy tells you to smile, he's sexually harassing you, right?"

Ariana was truly at the end of her rope, debating on whether or not she should tell the guy to stick a sock in it, but Jaclyn beat her to it.

She stepped forward and said, "As a matter of fact, it *is* super fucking annoying when men say that, so why don't you sit down and shut up already. People don't want to hear it."

The man looked surprised, but recovered quickly, glancing around the room again. "Oh, lookie here. Another one that wants to feel the burn." He paused, trying to think of something. "Sisterhood, right? What do you call that? Clits before shits?"

A bunch of the men laughed at that, but Jaclyn was undaunted. "You just burned yourself, moron. Perhaps you meant to say chicks before dicks?"

"Whatever. Fuck off."

Ariana moved to stand beside Jaclyn, giving the seated woman with the hurt wrist a quick nod. "Why don't you fuck off?" she said to the guy. "Take your misogynist crap back to your trailer park." And she didn't know why she added the last word, maybe because men like him got more enraged by it than pretty much anything else and what she wanted right then was to piss off this homophobic, sexist prick. "Faggot."

Jaclyn shot her a shocked, disapproving look. Ariana could only shrug, already biting her tongue, wishing she could take it back. What the hell was wrong with her? Internalized homophobia? Since when was that a thing with her?

Her plan, however ill-advised it had been, served its purpose. The guy's eyebrows shot up and for the first time, he looked truly pissed. The seated woman forgotten, he began walking towards Ariana, fists

94

balled. "What the fuck did you just call me, bitch?"

The rest of the waiting area had gone silent. No one was chuckling now. Instead, Ariana had dozens of furious male eyes boring into her from all angles. A couple other guys stood up, looking ready for anything. Were they planning to step in if the man with the broken nose became violent? She didn't think so. They had a look about them that only said one thing to her: lynch mob.

"Oh, shit," she muttered.

"We have to get out of here," Jaclyn said, quiet enough that only Ariana could hear. They turned, only to see two more men stepping up behind them.

"I asked you a question, cunt!" Broken nose douche barked.

Grabbing Jaclyn's hand, Ariana said, "I apologize in advance, babe."

"In advance of us being murdered in an emergency room. What the hell were you thinking?"

"I said I was sorry." She returned her attention to broken nose douche and said, "Blow me, twinkle toes."

With an wordless roar, the guy who really didn't enjoy being c
alled the other F-word raised his fist and swung.

13

The physical therapist still hadn't shown up and Bram knew it was unlikely that he'd see the person tonight. He was stuck.

Frustrated, he attempted to get out of the bed yet again, hoping the pain meds he'd received would make it easier, but now he was feeling too doped to do much of anything. It was ridiculous. Whoever heard of being forced to stay in a hospital due to broken bones? Certainly not him. And where the fuck was Fulton? Bram needed him, needed *someone* on his side.

He'd managed to swing his good leg off the bed, tipping over slightly before catching himself, when he heard screaming. Facing the inside of the room, his back to the door, he couldn't spin his neck far enough around to see into the hallway but then his door slammed and a panting male voice said, "Holy fuck, dude! They're killing him!"

Bram struggled to turn around on the bed. A young guy, probably in his twenties, was leaning with his back pressed against the door, sweat streaming down his face.

"What?" Bram asked. "Who?"

The guy was dressed in street clothes, so clearly not a patient in the hospital. A visitor?

"My grandfather! Oh, Jesus! They just started beating him!"

"Who? Who's beating him?"

"My mom and my aunt! They just snapped and when I tried to get between them and his bed, they came after me too. Just whaling on me! I got the fuck out there and asked a nurse to help. I begged her, but she just looked at me and . . . she smiled, man. She fucking smiled when I told her what they were doing to grandpa!" The guy, practically a kid, started bawling.

Bram wasn't overly surprised to hear the guy's story. It was fucked up, yeah, but seemed to be par for the course at the moment.

The kid ran over to the phone on the table by the bed.

"It doesn't work," Bram said, but the kid ignored him, dialing anyway.

When he realized he couldn't call out, he yelled, "Fuck!" Then, a horrified look came over his face and he raised his hand to his mouth, looking fearfully at the closed door. "*Shhh!*"

"Relax," Bram said. "I'm sure someone will help your grandfather." He didn't know if he believed his words or not—this place was a goddamn circus with a bunch of weirdos running it. "Do you think you could . . . I don't know . . . see if you can find me a wheelchair?"

"A what?" the guy looked at Bram as if seeing him for the first time. His eyes found the cast on his leg and his face fell. "Oh, shit. You can't walk?"

"I haven't been given the chance to try but I don't think so."

The sound of running footsteps passed the door and both men looked over with dread.

"I don't know what happened to my mom," the guy said once the sound had diminished. He began to weep. "I've never seen her so angry. Grandpa was talking about how Grandma always made him his favorite Black Forest cake for his birthday. With extra frosting. Then Aunt Ginny said how Grandma had always spoiled him. I thought she was kidding but when I looked at her, I knew. She wasn't kidding. She was *pissed*. She said he didn't deserve it, and that made *him* pissed and then he started talking about how Grandma had been a good wife but my mom said, 'you always treated her like a slave.' And it just got worse and worse until they started pummeling him." He wiped dripping snot from his upper lip with his shirt sleeve. "I tried to stop them."

Bram wasn't particularly interested in this story. He said, "That sucks, man. But . . . you think you could find me that wheelchair? I need to get to a phone. Unless . . . you don't happen to have one, do you?"

The guy shook his head. "It died, so I left it in my mom's car to charge. That's why I wanted yours to be working."

"Right." The meds must really be doing a number on his head. Bram had already forgotten the kid trying to use the phone. Everything was getting a bit swimmy. "Listen, please. I need to call someone before I pass out."

"Aaron!" A woman in the hallway shouted and the kid, obviously Aaron, shrunk back, bumping into the bed.

"Shit," he whispered. "That's my mom."

"How old are you?" Bram whispered back.

"Nineteen. Why?"

"Just making sure you're not a minor."

Aaron's mom shouted his name again. She sounded further away the second time. Aaron showed visible relief.

"So, how about it?"

"What?"

Bram sighed with impatience. "The wheelchair."

"I have no idea where they keep them. Besides, if my mom sees me . . . " He trailed off with a shudder.

"You can't hide from her forever."

"You wanna bet?"

"Aaron, come on. Just go to the desk and ask them." Bram thought about that for a second, then said, "Scratch that. Don't say anything. Just look around. They probably have one close by. Or maybe in a closet." He realized he knew very little about the inner operations of hospitals.

"She'll kill me," Aaron whined.

"Why? She's mad at your grandfather, not you."

"I shoved her when she wouldn't stop hitting him."

"I'm sure she'll understand. You were just trying to protect him. Did he have a heart attack or something?"

Aaron shook his head. "He had a hip replaced."

"Listen, just poke your head out, see if the coast is clear, and if it is, go look for it. It'll take two minutes, tops. It's not like I'm asking you to search the whole hospital. Just do a lap around the floor. If you see her coming, you can duck into a room, just like you did with this one."

The kid began chewing the cuticle of his thumb and Bram thought it was probably a substitute for sucking it. "I don't know," he said slowly.

"I'll give you fifty bucks."

Eyes widening, Aaron hesitated for the length of a heartbeat. "Deal."

"Go in that closet there and grab the bag. Hand me my wallet."

For the first time since this shitshow began, Bram felt a twinge of hope blossoming in his heart like spring wildflowers.

14

Drunk enough to admit things she'd only rarely said aloud before, Nicki, who'd moved from the couch to the floor, where Marge also sat, said, "I kissed my best friend Lisa in high school."

Shirley, still on the couch, poured the last of the Wild Turkey into Nicki's extended glass. "Oooo. That sounds like a juicy tale."

"I guess that makes me bi too, huh?" Nicki said and took a sip.

Marge stretched out of the floor, resting a half empty beer on her belly. "No."

"No?"

"No," Shirley agreed. "If every person who'd ever done anything with a person of the same sex was bi, the whole world would be bi."

"Maybe the whole world *is* bi," Nicki countered.

"You'd think," Shirley said. "To hear most women tell it."

"What do you mean?"

"Honey," Shirley said. "I have lived long enough to see gay girls pretending they're not to become straight girls pretending they're not. The latter usually to turn on the men in their lives."

"Oh, god," Marge said. "Let's not get started on that again."

"Agreed," Shirley said, and got wobbily to her feet. "I gotta hit the sack anyway."

"Noooo." Nicki was genuinely disappointed. "It's not even ten."

"I'm an old lady."

"You're only an old lady when it's convenient for you," Marge said. "Otherwise, you're younger than me."

"True. You girls behave. Nicki, don't kiss my daughter." She laughed and left the room, leaving the younger women embarrassed.

Marge sat up and chugged the rest of her beer, rolling the bottle across the floor. "Another dead soldier. The last one."

"We should go get more," Nicki said.

Staring forlornly at the empty bottle, Marge said, "We should. We can walk."

They got up, grabbed their jackets and headed out into the night, giggling and bumping into each other on the dark sidewalks canopied by trees just beginning to sprout buds.

The neighborhood was mostly quiet, though occasionally they could hear couples arguing, sometimes quite loudly, until Marge said, "Jesus. What's with people lately? Everyone is fighting with everyone."

"Not really," Nicki said. "Men are fighting with women."

"You think?"

"I know. Women are pissed off by how men treat them."

"Hmm. Well, no offense, but it's about fucking time."

"Lesbians have the right idea," Nicki said, laughing a little.

"Too bad so many straight people accuse us of being men haters though."

Nicki was surprised. "People say that to you?"

"Oh, yeah. Mostly guys though. They're too damn dumb to realize that straight women have always had more cause to hate them. It's the straight chicks who get treated like shit by guys."

Nicki pondered the statement but realized she was probably too drunk to think about it deeply at the moment.

They were still walking through the suburban neighborhood when the strobing red and blue lights of a police car illuminated the street, stopping just a few houses ahead of them. They watched as two officers emerged from the car even as a man ran out of the house, meeting the cops in the street.

"My girlfriend . . . " the man sobbed. "She came at me with a knife. I had to stop her."

Nicki and Marge froze in their tracks, mesmerized.

The cops, a male and a female, immediately reached for their weapons, but neither withdrew them.

"Take it easy," the male cope said. "Tell us what happened."

"Is your girlfriend still in the house?" the female asked.

"Yes," the guy said. "She's really hurt. Oh, fuck, oh, fuck, oh, fuck."

"Is she breathing?" the female asked.

"I . . . I don't know."

"Calm down," the male cop said as the female cop headed inside the house.

The cop kept trying to talk the guy down from his hysteria, keeping his hand on his weapon and glancing towards the house where his partner had gone. Nicki and Marge continued to watch, the liquor store they'd been headed to forgotten. The cop's voice was too quiet to hear for the most part, but they distinctly heard him say an ambulance was on the way, which was confirmed by the sound of distant sirens.

"We should get out of here," Marge whispered and started to continue up the street.

Nicki stopped her, grabbing her wrist. "Hold on." She didn't feel drunk anymore. Just curious, anxious to see how this gruesome little scene played out.

"This is fucking morbid," Marge said. "I can't believe it's just a few blocks from where I live."

After what seemed like forever, but in reality was probably less than two minutes, the female officer emerged from the house, her face stricken. As she marched down the walkway towards the street, Nicki recognized the stride immediately. She was pissed.

"Is she alive?" the guy asked.

"She is," the female officer said. "She said you attacked her after she confronted you about fucking around on her."

"What?" The guy started to stammer. "That's . . . that's . . . "

"Turn around!" She grabbed him by the shoulder and spun him, shoving him against the cruiser.

"That crazy bitch is lying," the guy shouted. "Fucking whore!"

The female officer didn't hesitate. She pulled out her weapon and shot the guy in the back of the head. From where Nicki and Marge stood, they were able to see his face explode outward in a chunky mist. The shot was so much louder than Nicki could have ever imagined a shot would be, and she stood frozen, Marge crying out in shock and gripping Nicki's arm hard enough to hurt.

The male officer shouted, started to draw his own weapon, presumably to aim it at his partner, but she didn't give him a chance. She turned and shot him in the face, dropping him instantly.

Marge flat out screamed then, causing the female officer to look directly at them. She paused, studying them briefly, and then walked around to the driver's side of the cruiser and drove away, turning off the roof lights and leaving the two bodies in the road.

"Oh, my fucking god," Marge said, speaking as though it was hard for her to breathe. "I'm gonna be sick."

Nicki felt a little queasy herself. She grabbed Marge by the hand and began dragging her back the way they'd come. She had a feeling hell was about to break loose and they should be inside when it did.

15

Mark sat on the bed in his psych ward room, an icepack pressed to his head above his left ear while the nurse—her name was June he'd learned—stood nearby, hands on hips, watching him with a scowl.

"Where's Patti?" he asked.

"Just down the hall. We gave her something to calm her nerves."

Mark wondered why he wasn't given anything to calm *his* nerves. "I don't like being in the same place with her."

"I'm sorry, but that's just the way it is for now. We're waiting for an empty bed on the other side to open up. In the meantime, we'll keep you separated so you don't upset her again."

"Upset *her*!" He got to his feet. "What about me! I'm the wronged party here! I was the one assaulted!

108

She stabbed me, for Christ's sake!"

"I need you to sit down and relax," June told him, holding up a hand.

He sat down immediately. "I'm sorry, but, this isn't right. She should be in jail."

"She was arrested last night and then brought here. It's the best thing for her at the moment."

"What was she arrested for?"

"That's not your concern. You just worry about yourself, okay?"

"I *am* worried about myself! I'm in a locked ward with the person who wants me dead!"

"Calm down." Her voice took on a tone of impatience. "Do you want to take something to settle your nerves?"

In truth, he felt like crying. How had his life become such a shitshow? One minute, everything was normal and the next . . . he was here. "No," he said. "I'm okay."

"Are you hungry?"

He considered. It was strange he hadn't thought about food much. He shrugged his shoulders like a pouting little boy.

"The sooner you eat something, the sooner you'll get out of here."

"Really?" He felt a stab of hope.

"That's not the only criteria but it's a step."

"What else do I have to do?"

"Once you get over to the other side, you'll assigned a psychiatrist. He or she will help you along that path."

"I want a man!" he said, too quickly, judging by her face.

"You'll get whoever is available, Mark." She glowered at him. "Now, would you like something to eat or not?"

"Will Patti be out there?"

She sighed heavily. "No."

"Okay, then. I guess I could eat."

"Hand me the icepack."

Standing up, he did as ordered and followed her out to the common area, nervously casting glances behind him, as he went, terrified Patti would sneak up behind him.

In the common room, he sat at the table and was given Salisbury steak, mashed potatoes, green beans and an apple cobbler for dessert and water to wash it all down. He felt like he was in grade school again.

Over in the recliner, Russell sat staring at the television and picking his teeth with a finger nail. A nature program was on, a TV crew following a tribe of monkeys.

June stood at the nurse's station with another nurse, talking softly but Mark was close enough to hear. Their conversation was more interesting to him than the TV program and he cocked his head slightly, though he kept his eyes on the television.

"It's just disgusting," June said. "I hope he dies

in prison."

"Better yet," the second nurse said. "Feed him to a tank of piranhas."

"No kidding," June nodded. "And you just know she wasn't the first he did this to. The other patients probably never came out of sedation long enough to realize they were being raped."

"I'm switching to a woman dentist. This stuff is just rampant. You can't trust men at all."

"Nope. I hope none of them got pregnant. Can you imagine?"

"Like I said . . . piranhas."

"Hopefully they'd eat his pecker first. Nice and slow so he has plenty of time to think about it."

"And feel every bite."

"Exactly."

The phone on the desk chimed and June gave her coworker a last head shake before answering it. The second nurse walked off, headed to another part of the wing.

Mark continued to eat, though his skin had broken out in gooseflesh and he didn't have much of an appetite.

The kid who'd pulled Patti off him wandered into the common room and sat at the table across from Mark. They nodded at each other as Russell shouted at the TV, causing June to give him a sharp look.

"None of that now," she said. "Or you go back to your room."

Russell piped down, wrapping his arms around himself while June said goodbye into the phone before turning her attention to the computer.

"He's never getting out of here," the kid said to Mark, barely above a whisper.

"Probably not," Mark agreed, also keeping his voice low. "I'm Mark, by the way."

"Danny."

Danny shot a quick look over at June, then asked, "What did you do to get locked up in here, man?"

"I don't even know at this point," Mark said, staring at his food. "Pissed off the wrong nurse I guess."

"Easy to do." When Mark said nothing, he went on. "That your old lady who attacked you?"

"Yeah." He looked up, surprised. "How did you know?"

"Heard the staff talking. Said you fucked with her so bad she lost her friggin' mind."

Mark dropped his spork. "They said that?"

Danny nodded, eyeing the food tray. "You gonna finish that?"

Shooting June a cautious glance, Mark pushed the tray across the table. "Help yourself." He'd lost what little appetite he'd had.

"Thanks, man." Danny dug into Mark's leftovers.

"What did you do?" Mark asked.

"Huh?"

"To get locked up in here."

"Oh." Danny swallowed the last bite of Salisbury

steak. "O.D."

Mark's eyebrows shot up. "On purpose?"

Shrugging with only one shoulder, Danny suddenly seemed more interested in the TV, so Mark decided not to ask any further questions. It didn't matter anyway.

Suddenly, June stood beside the table, giving Mark a disapproving look. "Not eating after all?"

Both Mark and Danny abruptly morphed into little boys caught doing something they knew would get them punished.

"I . . . I ate most of it," Mark told her.

She studied both of their faces for an uncomfortable amount of time before saying, "A bed opened up on the other side. Let's go get your things."

A wave of relief passed over Mark the likes of which he hadn't felt since learning his son's high fever broke when he was four and sick with a staph infection.

"I don't have any stuff," he said, standing up.

Impatiently, she said, "Didn't you get a toothbrush and other toiletries when you came in?"

"Oh. Yeah, I did."

"Well, go get them!"

Mark looked at Danny, who shrugged again. "Later, man."

"Later, man," Russell shouted, causing Mark to flinch.

Without replying, Mark hurried to do as he was

113

told, anxious to get as far away from both June and Patti as this damn place would allow.

16

Ariana and Jaclyn found that the hospital staff was too busy intervening in other altercations to pay theirs much mind.

They hurried towards the exit only to find the pathway blocked by more angry men who'd over-heard the shit go down. The women stopped and reversed direction, going deeper into the hospital, passing once more through the waiting area where men shouted obscenities at them when they were spotted.

"You better run, you fucking bitches," someone yelled.

Ariana resisted the urge to confront the yell-er, quickening her pace instead. Luckily, the men weren't following very fast, as if they were restrain-ing themselves, but just barely.

As they turned a corner, they witnessed a woman in a lab coat pummeling a male nurse, who was trying to grab hold of the doctor's wrists but failing miserably.

"This is the last time you talk to me like that," the doctor snarled, belting the guy in the head.

Tempted to stop, Ariana slowed down until Jaclyn grabbed her hand. "Ari, come on."

"What the hell is happening?" Ariana asked as they continued walking. She looked back over her shoulder and saw the guy with the broken nose rounding the corner. When their eyes met, he stopped walking, fixing her with a murderous glare. "Fuck. That asshole is following us."

"Elevator up ahead," Jaclyn said, pointing to a sign. "He won't know which floor we go to."

Only when they were at the elevator and had pushed the up button, did Ariana dare another look back.

The man, seeing their plan, began to rush towards them, pausing only to give the angry doctor a quick shove away from the male nurse.

The elevator dinged and slid open and they hurried inside, hoping it would close before the man reached them.

"Where you going, bitches?" he shouted. "I got something for you!"

Jaclyn's grip on Ariana's hand tightened to the point of pain and then the door slid closed. They both heaved sighs of relief and Jaclyn pushed the button for the top floor.

"Why did you do that?" Ariana asked. "We should be going down, not up."

"To the parking garage? Are you nuts? Those things are creepy on the best of days."

Jaclyn had a point. People were being assaulted in parking garages all the time, just due to them being so frequently secluded and empty.

When they reached the top floor, the elevator dinged again and they exited, walking straight into a young man pushing another guy in a wheelchair. The wheelchair-bound man had his right leg in a cast from toes to upper thigh, sticking straight out.

"Whoa," he said. "Careful."

"Sorry," Ariana said, weaving around him.

"If you're going down to the ground floor," Jaclyn told them, "I wouldn't."

Both of the men looked nervous. "Why not?" the wheelchair-bound man asked.

"It's chaos down there," Ariana said. "People fighting. Not sure what's going on, but yeah, be careful."

"It's no better here," the man said. "Even the staff is . . . uh . . . hostile."

"Yeah, we noticed," Jaclyn said.

"Well, how are we supposed to get out of here, then?" the older man asked, as the younger one kept looking around like he expected to be jumped by a monster. Ariana had to wonder what had happened to him to make him so fearful.

"Where do you think you're going?"

They all turned to see a nurse in floral scrubs walking briskly towards them, directing her question to the guy in the wheelchair.

"I'm leaving," he said, matching her antagonistic tone. "You can't keep me here. I'm sure there's laws preventing it and I'll sue your ass if you try to stop me."

"Will you now?" The nurse's face split into a grin Ariana found unnerving. She seemed truly delighted by the threat of a lawsuit. "You'll sue my ass." She let out a hearty laugh. "You're a pistol, Bram. You really are. Now let's get you back in bed."

"Fuck you," Bram spat.

"Wow," the nurse replied. "Such language. That's not really called for, now is it?"

It was clear to Ariana that these two had some sort of unfriendly history between them.

"I don't think you're yourself, Bram," the nurse continued. "I'm very worried about you." She looked Ariana and Jaclyn up and down. "Are you two part of Bram's family?"

Ariana opened her mouth to answer but before she could Jaclyn quickly said, "Yes, we're his sisters."

The nurse looked not only surprised, but also skeptical. "Is that right?"

"That's right," Jaclyn said, offering a little smile.

118

"Big brother . . . Bram."

"Uh huh," the nurse nodded. "And how did you know Bram was in here?"

"Aaron called them," Bram said quickly. "With his cell phone."

The younger guy blanched at this, leading Ariana to assume he was Aaron.

"Is that so?" the nurse said, her eyes scanning Aaron's face coldly.

"Yep," Bram said. "Now, if you don't mind, I'm getting out of here."

"Well, there's quite a bit of paperwork for you before you go," the nurse said. "And I already told you you have to consult with the physical therapist before we can release you."

"Fuck that," Bram said. "I'm leaving tonight. Right now."

"Rules are rules," the nurse said. She began to take hold of the wheelchair but Ariana stepped in front of her. "Excuse me!" she snapped, putting up an arm to block her but Ariana stood her ground. A stare down ensued and there was no telling how long it would have lasted if another women hadn't come down the hall and yelled, "Aaron! There you are!"

The younger man let out a yelp of fear and began to frantically press the down button on the elevator panel.

"Get over here!" the woman shouted, pointing at the floor in front of her as though she were talking to a puppy. By the look of the kid, Ariana thought he might actually tinkle on the floor like one as well.

"Get over there," the nurse said to Aaron in a sing-song voice.

The elevator dinged and the door opened, Aaron slipping inside and proceeding to punch buttons while peering out at the scolding woman.

Bram attempted to roll the wheelchair forward into the elevator, but the nurse quickly sidestepped and cut off his access.

"Move, bitch!" Bram struggled to wheel around her as the other woman began charging across the room to get to Aaron.

"Jesus," Jaclyn said, stepping aside.

The elevator closed a second before the woman reached it and she pounded on the steel briefly before demanding to know where the stairs were.

Everyone ignored her and she stomped off in search of them.

"You need to leave him alone," Jaclyn told the nurse. "Just back off."

"Back off?" the woman mocked. "I think I know my job, young lady."

Down the hall in one of the patient rooms, a man began to scream, diverting everyone's attention briefly and when the nurse made no move to see what was happening down there, Ariana said, "Shouldn't you go see what that's about?"

"Someone else can handle it."

"Obviously not. He's still screaming."

Amazingly, the nurse shrugged, returning her attention to Bram. "I *will* call security."

"Go for it," Jaclyn said. "We'll wait right here."

The nurse's eyes narrowed. "You all think you're pretty smart, don't you? I'm just trying to do my job."

"You're shitty at your job," Bram said. His words were punctuated by the screams coming from down the hall, which the nurse continued to ignore, too busy glaring at the trio, until a woman began to shriek in obvious pain. Only then did the nurse's face show concern. She pointed a stubby finger at Bram. "You don't move till I get back." She jogged away towards the screaming and the instant she was out of sight, Ariana pressed the elevator button.

"Let's get the fuck out of here."

17

When they were all in the elevator, the women who'd come inexplicably to his defense introduced themselves to Bram. He made a mental note to re-member which was which by establishing Jaclyn as the hotter of the two. She was taller, had long hair and a better figure. In different circumstances, he would have tried his hand with her but this wasn't the time and besides, he could tell the women were a couple. Ariana gave it away, being the more butch of the two.

"That chick is probably gonna get on the phone the second she sees we took off," Ariana said.

"No doubt," Jaclyn agreed. "We have to make sure we're out of here before then."

"Do either of you have a cellphone I can borrow?"

Bram asked.

"No," they said in unison, sounding somewhat impatient with the question, as though they were sick of hearing it.

The elevator stopped at the next floor and everyone on it tensed, expecting to see the nurse, somehow, when the door opened. Instead, a disheveled man with a crazed look rushed in, wielding a hypodermic needle. He instantly began screaming at the women, *"Getthefuckoff! Getthefuckoff! Getthefuckoff!"*

Rather than immediately obeying, they shrank against the back wall, eyes wide and alarmed.

The new man lunged at them with the needle like a fencer attacking his opponent but as they were behind Bram, he was unable to reach them.

"I'll fucking kill you! Get the fuck off!"

All three of them began talking at once, saying "take it easy" and "calm down" and "relax."

"Stay away from me!" the man screeched.

"Okay, okay," Ariana said, holding out both hands. "We'll get off. Just move out of the way and we'll go."

The newcomer had his free hand out, ensuring the elevator door didn't close and Bram quickly rolled himself off the elevator and into the hallway. The women followed, giving the needle-brandishing guy as wide a berth as possible, never taking their eyes off his weapon.

The man stepped into the elevator, jabbing at the

floor panel. Before the door closed, he burst into uncontrollable sobs, leaving the three of them dumbfounded.

The floor they'd gotten off on didn't seem to be a floor at all. It was merely a very small lobby with a red door at one end, secured with an electrical key card panel.

"What the fuck?" Bram said. "Is this, like, a secret staff only floor or something?"

The red door opened suddenly and a young woman with rat-nest hair and bare feet, dressed in maroon scrubs, emerged, saw the three of them and dropped her eyes to the floor, refusing to make eye contact. She pressed the down button on the elevator as the red door began to slowly swing closed. Ariana, who was closest to it, grabbed it and held it open for Bram, who wheeled through as quickly as he could.

Once they crossed the threshold, they entered a large room with about five circular tables on one side and a TV rec center/kitchen area on the other.

Everyone in there was dressed in the same maroon scrubs. About half a dozen of them, all seated at the tables, alone or in pairs. To the immediate right of the red door was a enclosed nursing station, unoccupied at the moment, and to the left and right, hallways, closed doors leading off them.

"Is this what I think it is?" Jaclyn asked.

"It's the psych ward," Ariana replied.

Some of the patients looked over at the three

newcomers with curiosity, while others didn't even glance up. One woman sat alone at a table, chin resting on her hand, as though she were asleep. Maybe she *was* asleep, for all Bram knew.

A nurse came out of a hallway to the right of the nursing station and entered the small locked room via a door on the other side of where Bram and the others were. It took the nurse several seconds before she noticed the trio, at which point she gasped and reached for something on the desk, causing the red door behind them to make an audible clicking sound.

Bram looked over his shoulder at the women he'd entered with, saw them exchange a glance which told him they knew what the click was as well as he did: the nurse had locked them in.

"Excuse me?" The nurse addressed them. "Can I help you?"

"We just . . . " Ariana started to say, but trailed off, clearly uncertain of how to continue.

Bram cleared his throat. "I think one of your patients just took off."

The nurse's eyes widened and she immediately grabbed a nearby telephone, turning her back to the room. From the little Bram could hear, it sounded like she already knew which patient it was.

"Hey."

A balding man had approached Bram, looking haggard, holding his belly protectively for some reason. He towered over Bram in his wheelchair. Tall and thin and pale, the guy looked like he'd seen better days.

"Hey, yourself," Bram said, doing his best to appear friendly. He figured he couldn't take any chances in the loony bin.

"What's going on outside?" the thin man asked. "Is it . . . normal?"

"Normal?"

"You know, like . . . uh . . . just . . . normal."

Bram studied the man's face carefully before glancing over at Ariana and Jaclyn, who only shrugged. The man waited for a reply, his eyes wide and anxious.

"Not really sure what you mean by normal," Bram said, finally. "And I haven't been outside. But in this damn hospital? No. Nothing is normal."

"Bram." Jaclyn put a hand on his shoulder. "Maybe you shouldn't—"

"It's okay," the tall man said. He lowered his voice. "I'm not really crazy."

"Right," Bram said. "I didn't think you were."

"Really. I'm not. My name is Mark Gray." He lifted his scrub shirt, revealing angry-looking puncture wounds in his abdomen and chest. "My wife did this to me," he said, as if that would for sure let everyone know he was, in fact, not crazy.

"That's gotta suck," Bram said, backing up the wheelchair a bit.

"I don't even know why," Mark said. "She just went nuts." He paused, dropped his shirt back into place, and looked warily at the lesbians behind Bram, then stooped a little, putting his face closer to Bram's. "That's why I asked if everything was normal outside. It's just that . . . I don't know. Women seem to . . . they seem to really hate me all of a sudden."

Bram blinked, rubbing a hand over his stubbled cheek.

Ariana stepped forward and Mark let out a squeak of fear, backing away. "It's not just women hating men," she said. "It's men hating women too."

"What?" Bram craned his neck to look at her. "No. I've only seen women being psychotic bitches." He quickly looked at Mark and around him at the other patients. "No offense."

"It's true, it's true." Mark nodded vehemently. "It's like they're all PMSing at the same time!"

Jaclyn laughed without humor, rolling her eyes. "Get a new line, for fuck sake."

"Men have always hated women," Ariana said. "Maybe men just aren't used to being hated back."

"What?" Bram said, incredulous. "That's not true. Most men love women!"

The lesbians looked at each other and cracked up, causing Bram to frown. What did they know? Of course they'd think that, since they probably hated men themselves.

"Excuse me," the nurse in the enclosed area said loudly, to get their attention. "Are you three visiting someone? You can't be in here otherwise."

"No," Ariana said. "We'll leave."

Bram thought of the nurse on the other floor and quickly said, "I am. I'm visiting . . . uh . . . "

"Mark," Mark said.

"Right." Bram snapped his fingers. "I'm visiting Mark."

The nurse, by her expression, knew he was lying but was distracted when a female patient came running down a hallway, shouting, "Call the police! Call the police!"

Unfazed, the nurse gave the young woman a bored look. "What's wrong, Jill?"

"Douglas and Christine are killing each other!"

The nurse came out of her locked enclosure. As she passed by, she told Bram and the others, "I'll be right back."

Mark gave Bram a knowing nod and Bram nodded back. "Crazy bitches."

18

Other people came outside to see what the commotion was about concerning the dead bodies in the road. Some people screamed, while others just stood, shocked into silence. Others took out their phones and took pictures or videos or both. Some seemed positively giddy with excitement. Nothing like this ever happened on this sleepy street.

Marge didn't seem to be aware of any of this, but Nicki took it all in as they hurried back to Marge's house. She was curious about people's reactions to the violence, fascinated by how different people responded to something so horrific. She wondered how they would respond to her own act of violence the night before, which apparently she'd so far gotten away with. She could only assume it was because the world seemed to be infected with some strange new madness, though she knew the symptoms had been building for years now. She knew this because she'd felt it in herself and seen it growing on the internet and on social media in particular. The more strides towards equality women made, the angrier men became. For some reason, men felt threatened by the shift, as though there was only so much equality to go around and if women had any of it, theirs would diminish. It was absurd of course, but, Nicki knew from experience, men were not particularly rational when they felt threatened because they hadn't lived their entire lives feeling threatened in the way women had. For women, it was a fact of life—someone, somewhere, wanted something from you, and if you weren't willing to give it freely, then they would take it by force and probably punish you for resisting in the first place. Now, finally, women were wising up and men were enraged, showing their true colors where they felt safest doing so: online. They now freely insulted and threatened women, emboldened by each other to keep upping the ante to see who could be the most offensive towards women in the hopes they could 'put women back in their place,' as it were. They were becoming increasingly desperate in their attempts to dominate women and the world and the more women pushed back, the angrier they became.

And vice versa.

Women were not about to go back to the kitchen.

Not in this lifetime—not in any lifetime.

Thinking about this as she hurried up the street with her friend, Nicki had to smile. It made her happy to know that men were being driven mad with rage towards women but also that women were finally fighting back. And this was the result. She knew that female cop back there had had enough, just as she had had enough last night in the drugstore.

It was a reckoning and she was part of it.

The knowledge made her feel gleeful and she had a hard time concealing her delight, wanting to shout with joy but knowing now was not the time. She would celebrate later.

When she and Marge arrived back at Marge's house, Marge went to wake up Shirley. By then, the night was alive with sirens and dancing red and blue police and ambulance lights. Nicki was disappointed, knowing that the female officer would surely be caught and probably shot dead long before ever seeing the inside of a courtroom, but still, she'd taken out a couple guys and to Nicki, that made the woman a legend. If every woman could kill two men, she thought, the world could finally be a fair and just place.

Smiling, she sank down into the couch, wishing they'd made it to the liquor store so she could revel now instead of later when she was alone.

No matter. Later would be just as good, if not better.

Dragged out of bed by Marge, Shirley came into the living room, groggy and confused, but clearly alarmed by what her daughter had told her and the sound of sirens filling the night. She sat down beside Nicki and hugged her tight.

"I'm so sorry you had to see that," Shirley said. "You must be so upset. I can't even imagine."

"Yeah," Nicki said. "It was . . . awful."

Marge had pushed aside the living room curtain and was peering down into the street as emergency vehicles raced by, headed to the scene of the shooting. "Oh, my god," she said. "So many people are going out there to see what's happening."

"Oh, no!" Shirley pressed her fingers to her lips. "I wonder if we should go out there and tell them not to go down there. They don't want that in their heads forever. It's bad enough you two had to see it. Everyone will have nightmares."

Nicki doubted she was going to have any nightmares but she kept her mouth shut on the matter.

"That's a bad idea, Mom," Marge said, letting the curtain fall back into place and turning to them. "Like Nicki said, it's probably going to get worse."

"Worse?" Shirley said. "How could it possibly get worse?"

"Just a feeling in the air. A tension."

"I'm sure you just think that because you're traumatized, honey." Shirley leapt off the couch and wrapped her arms around her daughter. "I'm so sorry you had to see and experience that. It's just horrifying."

While they talked, Nicki examined her nails, wondering how many people were already talking about the shooting online. Probably dozens. If they were in the neighborhood, they were aware of it, unless they slept like the dead. She thought more about the officer who'd done the shooting, wishing she could speak to her. She wondered if the cop would tell the truth about what had happened, if she were given the chance, and what the woman inside the house had said to her to make her come out and execute the man in the street. It was a fascinating puzzle, as far as Nicki was concerned, and she looked forward to learning more of the details.

Outside, people began shouting, glass shattered somewhere close by and a car alarm began to sound.

"Shit!" Marge raced to the window to peer out again and Nicki jumped up to join her. Illuminated by a streetlamp, a woman wielding an aluminum baseball bat smashed the windows of a car while yelling at a man who stood nearby, screaming at her to stop as the alarm whooped.

"Fuck you, George!" the woman shouted to be heard, shattering another window. "Give yourself a fucking blowjob if you think it tastes so fucking great!"

Nicki couldn't help it—she burst out laughing, causing Marge to shoot her a sharp look.

"This is why feminism is cancer!" the man shouted back. At that, the woman ceased beating on the car and went after the guy with her bat. He took off running, shouting over his shoulder while she gave chase, screaming like an enraged banshee.

"Holy fuck," Marge said.

"I guess he shouldn't have pushed his luck," Nicki said, still snickering.

"She might kill him, Nicki! This isn't funny!"

Nicki bit her tongue, because, in fact, it *was* pretty funny. Instead of saying so, however, she said, "The guy just yelled feminism is cancer. What did he think was gonna happen?"

Shirley stood nearby, her face incredulous. "Is *that* what he was yelling?"

They both nodded.

"In that case," Shirley said, "I'm with Nicki. What did he expect?"

"Mom!" Marge gasped. When Shirley just shrugged, Marge continued. "Those are just words. You can't physically attack someone for something stupid they say."

"Apparently, you can," Nicki said, turning away from the window. "And if I was a guy right about now, I'd be smart enough to shut the fuck up for a change."

But, she wasn't a guy and though she didn't say it, she secretly hoped the idiots *did* keep running off at the mouth. Evidently, the time had come for them to learn their lessons and Nicki wanted a first row view for as much of it as possible.

Amid protests from both Marge and Shirley, she left the house a few minutes later, anxious to explore the night and be part of what she was sure was the beginning of a long overdue revolution.

19

Being on the other half of the psych ward was only slightly better than on the so-called Dark Side, as far as Mark was concerned. There were more people and most of them were doped to the gills, which seemed like a good thing, as no one was particularly combative, and there were more things to do, such as watching TV, reading or playing games like Uno or doing puzzles, but almost the entire day was taken up by group therapy sessions, one after the other, which he was uncomfortable with.

When the two woman came in with the guy in the wheelchair, Mark seized the opportunity to talk to them, asking what was happening out in the world.

As soon as the nurse tending the front desk disappeared down the hall, leaving the common area unattended for a time, Mark immediately leapt over the counter and began frantically searching for the button that would unlock the red door and lead to freedom.

"Got it," he said to Ariana. "When I hit this, hold that door open."

"Is that a good idea?" she said. "I mean, aren't you supposed to stay in here?"

"I don't fucking want to stay in here," Bram said. "Hit the button."

Mark did. The door clicked to unlocked and Ariana did as asked. Mark climbed back over the counter and went into the hall, followed by the trio of newcomers. They quickly shut it again when another patient got up from her table and tried to follow them out. There was no sense in letting a bunch of unstable people run loose.

Jaclyn hit the down button on the elevator and Mark stared up at the digital display, fidgeting nervously, praying it would arrive before the nurse returned and noticed his escape.

Someone on the other side of the red door began pounding on it, shouting, "Let me out!"

If there had been stairs to take, Mark would have taken them, but the stairs could only be accessed from within the locked ward and, of course, those doors were also locked. He chewed his lower lip anxiously, certain the elevator car would never arrive, and then it did.

Everyone waited for Bram to enter before stepping inside themselves. Once inside, Mark pressed the P on the panel. With any luck, when the nurse came back to the front, she would simply assume Mark and his visitors had all gone to his room, which was down the opposite hall where she'd been called to, hopefully buying him more time still.

Both Ariana and Jaclyn eyed him warily, as though he might be dangerous, and he supposed he couldn't blame them. Bram seemed completely indifferent, also just wanting out of the hospital.

"How do you plan on getting out of here when you're dressed like that?" Ariana asked him.

Mark looked down at himself, still dressed in the maroon scrubs, realizing for the first time that his feet were bare. "Shit. I didn't think of that."

Bram grunted. "You're lucky. I'm in this goddamn johnny, bare-assed."

"This is what we're doing now?" Jaclyn asked Ariana. "Smuggling men out of the hospital?"

"We're just riding the elevator. What they do in the parking garage is up to them," Ariana said.

"I hope this isn't illegal," Jaclyn replied.

Two floors down, when the elevator stopped and the door slid open, all four of them tensed up until an elderly woman peered in at them, paying Bram special attention. "I'll get the next one," she told them and no one argued. It didn't stop again until it reached the underground parking garage.

Again, Bram was allowed to go first and when

they'd all exited, it was Bram who said, "You ladies have a car?"

The women exchanged a glance and Jaclyn said, "No," too quickly. It was obvious to both men she was lying. Mark didn't intend to push it, but Bram said, "Come on. Don't bullshit us. I'm in a goddamn wheelchair." When the women didn't seem convinced, he asked if they at least had a cellphone he could borrow, which made them look even more annoyed.

"Why does everyone keep asking us that?" Jaclyn wanted to know. "Don't you guys have your own phones?"

"Obviously not," Bram said, an edge of anger in his voice.

Mark stood by awkwardly, somewhat afraid of what the women might do if provoked. He glanced up and down the parking garage, accessing where he could run if they decided to attack. Being barefoot made him nervous, knowing that their shoes gave them an advantage.

"Why the hell is it such a big deal?" Bram demanded. "It's one phone call."

"We don't carry phones," Ariana said.

"Whatever," Bram said, making it clear he didn't believe her. He began to wheel himself away, his broken leg sticking straight out. Then he stopped, looking around. "Which way is the damn exit?"

"You're going the right way," Jaclyn said.

Bram spun his wheelchair around, his face darkening. "You don't have to give me an attitude."

"What?" She frowned. "I'm not giving you an attitude. I just said you're going the right way, which you are."

"I have *had it* with bitches today," Bram suddenly shouted, his voice echoing through the garage. "Why can't you ever just do what you're told?"

"Excuse me?" Furious, Jaclyn took a step towards him.

"Whoa!" Ariana held up her hands. "Everyone, just calm down."

"I'm not gonna calm down," Jaclyn said. "He just fucking called us bitches!"

"He's under stress. Just ignore him."

"Under stress? Are you fucking kidding me right now?"

"How about you both shut the fuck up?" Bram said.

Another voice came from out of the shadows. "Maybe it's you who needs to shut the fuck up, you vile piece of fucking shit."

They all turned to see a woman approaching, striding quickly towards them, full of purpose. Mark had to squint at first, but as she drew closer, he could feel his testicles begin to crawl up into his body.

The woman coming towards them raised her right hand from her side and Mark saw the gun she held, though he had no idea what kind it was. If pressed, all he could have said was that it was black.

"Move and I'll blow your fucking heads off," the woman said.

She meant it. Mark could see that in her eyes instantly, the moment she was close enough. The world began to teeter, his stomach rolled and he suddenly was unsure if he could remain upright. Battling gravity suddenly seemed to take a tremendous amount of effort and he wasn't sure it was worth it.

As if from very far away, he heard Bram say, "Are you fucking kidding me?"

The gunshot was deafening and Mark fell into a crouch, covering his ears with his hands. When he next opened his eyes, he saw Bram was now missing part of his skull, his chin rested against his chest, his head fallen forward, spilling its contents down the front of his johnny and puddling on his lap.

The woman with the gun gave the corpse a half smile and said, "Play around, lay around, mother-fucker."

Mark turned his body away and began to vomit onto his own bare feet.

20

There was a moment when Ariana thought her own head had exploded, sure that thunder had split it apart, but it was the asshole in the wheelchair—Bram—who was dead. She looked from his body to Jaclyn, who was now gripping her upper arm hard enough to leave bruises, trying to drag her off, to Mark, cowering in a crouched position on the ground, puking and covering his head simultaneously, to the woman with the gun.

The same woman from the ER, who now stood smiling at her expectantly, as if expecting praise for the murder she'd just committed. Not seeing what she wanted, the woman's smile faltered and she swung the pistol towards Mark.

"*No!*" Ariana shouted. "No, please. No, no! Don't shoot him!"

The woman looked back at Ariana curiously. "Why not?"

"Just . . . just don't." She was aware she was begging in a way she'd never begged for anything. She sounded weak and terrified and pathetic. Jaclyn was crying softly as she did her best to yank Ariana away.

"Do you know him?" the woman asked. "He's not who you came here with."

"I . . . " She trailed off, with no idea what she could say to save his life. "He's . . . my brother."

The woman's eyebrows shot up. "Your *brother*? Somehow, I doubt that."

Ariana drew a blank. She didn't want to risk pissing this psycho off.

"Ari, come on," Jaclyn pleaded.

"He's probably still a rapist," the woman said. Her tone was conversational, as though they weren't all listening to the sound of blood and brains dripping onto the concrete in thick splats. "I mean, they're *all* rapists. If they're old enough to get hardons, right? And even if they're not, it's only because they're too chicken shit to do it. Scared they'll get caught. But they all want to. Every fucking one of them. Even brothers. Fathers. Husbands. Sons. If the dick works, they want to stick it wherever you don't want it stuck. Every fucking time. That's why there's so much incest nowadays. There's a hole. They just gotta stick it in there, they don't give a shit who it belongs to. Every hole is theirs."

While the woman ranted, her eyes on Mark, Ariana looked around. Her car wasn't far. She wasn't good with distance, but maybe thirty yards. Just a couple rows over from where they stood now. If she walked just a little way towards the exit, she'd probably be able to see it.

"Did you know," the woman said, looking back at Ariana again. "That lady scientist who took the first picture of the black hole, she's in hiding now. Did you know that?"

Slowly, Ariana shook her head.

"It's true. You want to know why? Because of fucking men, that's why. They just couldn't accept that a woman did something like that. Said it was bullshit. So, they harassed her. Sent her death threats. *Rape* threats. Because *of course*. That's where they just *have* to go. All because their fragile little egos can't stand the thought of a woman doing something amazing. Something they themselves would never be able to do." The woman focused on Mark again. Mark had dared a glance over his shoulder just as she was turning back to him. He yelped like a kicked puppy, covering his head again.

While the woman's attention was on Mark, Ariana backed up a few steps, taking Jac with her. She tried not to look at Bram as she got closer to the wheelchair but her eyes were drawn to the body anyway. Nearly gagging, she looked away, stepping

144

past it, trying to avoid the growing puddle of blood and brain matter.

The woman seemed to be enjoying Mark's terror and she laughed when she noticed he'd pissed himself. "Aw, is poor baby boy scared?" she taunted. "You're not the one in power, are you? That must be awful, huh? You've never known what it was like, have you? Never had any reason to be scared. White and male. American. I assume straight. You won the lottery before you left the womb, didn't you? Now what's happening? Do you feel like you're the low rung of the ladder? Bottom of the totem pole? Weak and helpless? Someone doing something to you you don't like? Tough shit, princess. Welcome to the new world."

"Please," Mark sobbed. "I didn't do anything to you."

"No?" The woman stepped closer to him, spurred on by his words. "Then who? Because you did something to someone. Your kind can't help it. It's your nature to be abusive. You're worse than animals. You're monsters."

"I . . . I have children," he said, almost too quiet to hear.

"Boys?"

He didn't reply, which Ariana thought was good. He needed to stop talking altogether but at least he was distracting her. Taking another couple steps back, Jaclyn behind her, Ariana positioned herself just behind the wheelchair, a little to its right.

"Answer me, motherfucker!" the woman shouted.

Mark squeaked in terror, covering his head with his arms as much as he could, trying to make himself as small as possible as Ariana tensed, fully expecting the woman to shoot him in that moment.

From elsewhere in the parking garage, a car engine roared to life, startling them all and causing the woman to look up, away from all of them. Ariana shoved the wheelchair towards her as hard as she could. It shot forward, Bram's casted leg sticking straight out, catching the woman in the thigh, knocking her off balance. She yelled, spinning towards Ari and Jaclyn, the weapon discharging near their feet, shooting fragments of concrete into the air.

"*Run,*" Ariana screamed at Jaclyn and they both bolted between a row of cars, out of the line of fire and kept running, hunched over, towards the car. She knew she'd just signed Mark's death warrant, but survival instinct had taken over. Behind them, the woman was shouting, and the gun fired again. Ariana flinched, expecting her own head to blow apart the way Bram's had, but it didn't, and she kept moving towards her own car, already fumbling in her pocket for the keys as she ran. Another two gunshots echoed through the garage as they reached the car. Ariana's hands were shaking so badly, she nearly dropped the keys, but she pressed the unlock button on the fob and the doors clicked. They both leapt inside, slamming the doors and Ariana started the engine, still hunched over. Jaclyn was crying freely now. Tires screeching, Ariana stomped on the gas and aimed the car for the exit, which was within sight. They were almost safe. So close.

From between two cars, Mark ran out into their path and Ari had to slam on the brakes to keep from running him over. She was relieved he was alive and appeared to be unhurt but her heart sank when he pointed the gun directly at her.

"Give me the car!" he screamed, still crying. "Get the fuck out!"

"Reverse!" Jaclyn shouted but Ari knew she couldn't reverse fast enough to avoid a bullet. Holding her hands above the wheel, she only knew she *couldn't* let him take the car but neither did she have the stomach to slam into him with it.

"*Ari! Drive!*"

Mark walked forward, still aiming the gun, though his hand was badly trembling. He stopped at the hood and only then could Ariana see the specks of blood freckling his face, arm and hand. Not his blood, she knew.

"I'll take you wherever you want to go," she called to Mark without thinking. She hadn't even known she was going to say the words and then they were out.

"Are you out of your fucking mind?" Jaclyn cried.

"Just *go!*"

But Ariana could see uncertainty in Mark's face. What he'd done, he hadn't wanted to do. It was self-preservation, and she suspected that what he was doing now was the same.

"We're not enemies," she went on, shocked that now she was crying too. "I swear to you, Mark. You don't have to do this."

He wavered. She saw it in his eyes and for some reason, she wondered if he was thinking about his children. How maybe, in his mind, he'd had to kill someone in self-defense, but that was different. He didn't have to do it again. Not now. Not to them.

Wracked with sobs, he lowered the gun. Not completely, and Ari doubted he did it on purpose, but at least it was pointed off to the side now, not directly at her.

"Please," she begged. "Just get in the car."

And much to her amazement, he did, getting into the backseat and falling over, wailing.

Jaclyn stared at her in disbelief and Ariana could shake her head. She took her foot off the brake and they left the garage, driving into the chaotic night, all three of them crying and shell-shocked, barely able see through the tears.

21

Nicki walked slowly down the street. On her right was a burning house, a cluster of people standing around, illuminated by firelight, crowding the area. As she drew nearer, they all turned to look at her and she realized they were all females of varying ages, including a small child sucking her thumb, being held presumably by her mother.

The small crowd squinted at her and Nicki knew they were determining her gender and only then did they step aside and allow her passage.

The night was alive with chaos and Nicki's body thrummed with the excitement of it all. She was happy to be out in it, to feel it against her skin, not be cooped up watching the events unfold on the news as she knew many people were. Continuing on, she grinned, breathing in the electric air.

The sound of sirens, near and far, was a constant but she took heart knowing there would never be enough of *them* to overwhelm the abundance of *us*.

She'd walked only a block when she happened upon the first abandoned corpse of a man, the body strewn across the sidewalk, so badly beaten it was impossible to tell what it had looked like while alive. If not for its nakedness, even determining sex would have been difficult but the gaping, unnatural wound in the crotch told her it had been mutilated. She could only hope it happened while it had been alive.

Strolling on, she witnessed a man, barely conscious, also nude, being strung up into a tree, a noose fashioned from an extension cord wrapped around its throat. The three woman committing the act gave Nicki a cursory glance, pausing for the briefest of moments, before turning away, disinterested in her, and returning their attention to the task at hand.

Nicki smiled, said, "Good job," and kept walking through the residential neighborhood.

It amazed and delighted her how quickly the revolution had begun. The fact that men hadn't seen it coming, she knew, was what spurned it on. They were too comfortable, thinking they could be as abusive as they wished, whether it was in person or in media or online. In business or in bedrooms. In the street or in the White House. They'd underestimated not only the power of women but the rage they were instilling in them. Essentially, they'd asked for this. Begged for it. And now it was theirs, in all its bloody glory. Castrated and gutted and flayed. All of it. Burned and broken and butchered. It was long, long overdue.

As she strolled, Nicki happened across an abandoned crowbar, which she snatched up, hefting its weight in her hand. It felt good. Great, even. Much better than the champagne bottle had felt at work the previous night. Much more natural. When she felt the tackiness of the iron, she saw it was still sticky with someone's blood but that was okay. She didn't suppose it was a woman's blood.

She'd traveled another block when a teenage male came running out of the dark towards her. Its face was panicked, slick with sweat and blood from an open gash over its left eye. She stepped to the side as though about to let it pass without interference but at the last second, she stuck out her foot and sent it sprawling face first into the sidewalk. Without hesitation, once it was down, she raised the crowbar and, with every ounce of her strength, she hit it, connecting with a shoulder blade. Even in the loudness of the evening, she still heard a crack, and though it had previously been silent, it started to scream. Satisfied, she did it again, and then again, careful not to hit it in the head because she didn't want to kill it. Not yet.

A teenage girl ran up, out of breath, and stopped to observe the scene. Nicki and the girl locked eyes and then the girl smiled at her. "Thanks," she said, waving a kitchen knife showily. "Fucker is too fast."

"Not anymore," Nicki told her. "Enjoy." She presented the writhing body with a flourish of her arm and went on her way, barely aware of the shrieking that began in her wake, already anxious to see what else this beautiful night had in store for her.

As she strolled, she swung the crowbar around, feeling a bit like Gene Kelly with his umbrella in *Singing in the Rain.* What a glorious feeling.

She was headed towards downtown and though the traffic grew busier, it seemed more things were happening indoors, which was a bit disappointing. She supposed it might have to do with being closer to police stations but she wasn't sure. Regardless, she decided to help herself to some of the festivities taking place behind closed doors, namely by peering through the windows of first floor dwellings. It took several attempts before she found anything that she found interesting enough to watch for more than a minute or so.

Inside one apartment on the corner of an intersection, a kitchen window blind was at half mast and inside, a balding and chubby naked man was bent over a table, its ankles and wrists fastened to the legs with strings of Christmas lights and what appeared to be dingy men's underwear shoved into its mouth. Nicki was afforded a sideview, so she couldn't see its starfish, specifically, which was kind of a shame, given the amount of blood running down the inside of its legs and the level of pain displayed on its face. Its eyes were squinched shut, perspiration beading on its forehead, snot dribbling from its nose as its fat cheek pressed into the tabletop.

Behind it, a woman removed a curling iron from its asshole and Nicki heard her say, "Shit. Need to plug it in again."

"That's okay," a second woman said. "Back to the Mag-Lite for now."

"I don't know." The first woman shook her head slowly, studying their handiwork. "I think he's warmed up for the rolling pin."

They both cackled madly and from her place in the shrubs, Nicki giggled along with them, wishing the window was open. Even a crack would have made it easier to hear.

Upon mention of the rolling pin, its eyes shot open and it began to thrash around, struggling against its restraints. Despite its panic, its eyes connected with Nicki's, wide and pleading. It knew she was there. She smiled and offered it a little wave as the second woman reached for the rolling pin on the counter by the stove.

As the woman approached, Nicki felt an almost orgasmic shudder through her body. She leaned in closer to the window, cupping her hands against the glass to cut any glare and get a better view.

Behind her on the street, tires screeched, a horn blared and the earsplitting crunch of metal colliding with metal and glass shattering caused her to flinch and spin around to see the mangled ruins of a car T-boned by another, larger car.

All was silence for a moment, as if the city itself gasped or skipped a beat. Or was that just in Nicki's head?

The scene in the kitchen forgotten, she clambered out of the shrubs and slowly walked towards the car wreck. Before she reached it, a male voice from the larger car began to wail and a woman opened the driver's side door. She didn't step out as much as she fell out, stumbling, a hand pressed to the center of her face, blood seeping out from between her fingers. The woman looked around, dazed, before turning back to the car. "Jac?"

Nicki assumed she was speaking to the male inside. In the other car, another male was draped over the steering wheel at an angle. It wasn't moving and as far as Nicki could tell, it wasn't breathing either.

"Jac!" The woman shouted, running around to the other side of the car, her broken nose evidently forgotten. She yanked open the passenger door and pulled out another woman, who appeared to be mostly okay, though very stunned.

Nicki was happy to see that Jac was female but the male wailing inside the car continued. Both women saw her and the first one asked if she had a phone. Nicki shook her head, pausing briefly in the street to look over her shoulder, sensing eyes on her. One of the women she'd been watching had come outside, rolling pin still in hand.

"Are they okay?" she called over.

"Looks like," Nicki replied.

When she got to the car, she peered inside to see the wailer. It held its head in its hands, rocking back and forth. Nicki made a disgusted face before returning her attention to the women who'd escaped the wreck. They were now hugging in the street and looking over at the dead male in the demolished car. It had been it who'd bombed through the intersection and Nicki supposed if it came down to it, she'd testify that it had been the careless driver in the wrong, but she doubted it ever would. Not with the way the world was now.

Other cars coasted by, pale faces staring at the accident. Whenever Nicki saw that one of the staring faces was male, she made a show of waving the crowbar, encouraging them to move along, which they all did, giving their vehicles a sudden burst of gas.

"What are you doing?" one of the women asked, sniffing and wiping away tears. She was not the one named Jac.

"Helping you," Nicki said, nonchalantly. She smiled broadly at the two women, before focusing on the backseat passenger once more.

22

Mark was not himself.

He lay across the backseat, tears streaming from his eyes, sobbing in a way he couldn't remember ever having sobbed before. Not even as a child.

There were only two thoughts in his head: first, that he'd killed someone; and second, of his children, both of whom he desperately wanted to see. What would they think upon learning their dad was a murderer? Would they understand it had been in self-defense? They would, he knew, to some degree, but would they look at him differently? Would they *think* of him differently? He thought they probably would. Who wouldn't? Because he already thought of himself differently. He'd blown apart that woman's face, just as she'd blown apart Bram's, and he'd been horrified, the second murder far worse than the first.

She would have killed you too.

He knew it was true. But still, he wept. He'd never been a religious man and now he supposed he never would be. He wasn't sure why he thought that. Because how could any god love him? Probably.

They'd been in the car for roughly five minutes when Jaclyn turned on the radio. The news, they learned, was not good.

He had been aware of the current trend of men and boys being acquitted of violent crimes against women—nearly everyone was aware of it. It seemed, however, that the latest several—a college student from a well-known affluent family, a Hollywood producer, and a high-ranking politician—had been the last straw for the general populace of young to middle-aged women. Not only were they rioting and destroying property but they'd also become unpredictable and violent. The newscaster said multiple murders had already been committed all over the country, overwhelming police forces, and states of emergency had been declared. In solidarity, women in Europe were also wreaking havoc and rage was expected to hit Asia within a matter of hours.

Mark thought of his daughter. Always his precious one, they'd been incredibly close since she was tiny. Daddy's girl. Now he wondered if she would try to kill him if given the chance, or if she was trying to kill some other guy, who in turn would murder her out of self-defense, just as Mark had had to do.

And what of his son? Was he fleeing for his life from an enraged mob of women? Mark couldn't imagine a scenario where both of his kids came out of this nightmare in one piece. The images flashing through his mind made him sob harder.

"Please take me to my house," he said,

after catching his breath for a moment. "I need to call my kids."

"You can call them from a payphone," Ariana replied, swerving the car around something in the road. Mark was sure he didn't want to know what it was, but the flickering light falling into the backseat let him know whatever it had been, it was burning. It seemed like a lot of the city was burning now.

"I don't have their numbers memorized," he sniffed. "No one has numbers memorized anymore."

Ariana sighed. "For fuck sake. Where do you live?"

Mark gave her the address.

"Are you fucking kidding me? That's on the other side of the city!"

"Ari," Jaclyn said. "Calm down."

"How can you say that? How do you expect me to calm down right now?"

When he went to wipe his trickling nose with the back of his hand was when Mark remembered he was still holding the gun. He sat up and pointed it in Ariana's general direction. *"Just fucking take me!"*

She quickly glanced over her shoulder, her eyes narrowing, before returning her attention to the road. "You fucking prick," she said through clenched teeth.

Something in him snapped. *"Fuck you!"* he screamed, leaning forward to get as close to her ear as possible. *"Fuck all of you fucking bitches! You're all fucking crazy whores! Why is it so hard for you to just give me fucking blowjob once in a while? I work all day to take care of this fucking family and you're* never *grateful! All you do is fucking bitch at me! Make us take turns cooking? Really, Patti? That's not how it's supposed to be! You're supposed to take care of me like a fucking* wife! *Just do what you're fucking told once in a fucking while! You complete fucking* cunt!*"*

Suddenly Ariana slammed on the brakes, launching Mark forward between the two front seats to bounce off the dashboard and back again, the gun tumbling from his hand to god only knew where. One of the women—he thought it was Jaclyn—cried out in fear as the car skidded forward on locked tires. Mark barely had time to comprehend what was happening when they crashed into another car, sending him flailing, stunned, confused and in pain, a new knot already welling up on his forehead.

23

Ariana had a splitting headache and had wrenched her shoulder and her neck. Every time she glanced over at the dead guy, a fresh wave of nausea assaulted her. She leaned on Jaclyn, doing her best not to break down completely. But that was exactly what she wanted to do. Just find a place to collapse and sob, probably for the rest of the night, however long that would be.

They hadn't driven very far from the hospital but it had been far enough to know the city was in chaos. According to the radio, what was happening wasn't an isolated event. Cities all over the country were in turmoil. She knew now that not paying any attention to the news—that silly pact she'd made with her girlfriend so long ago—had been a huge mistake, though she wondered if she, or anyone, could have predicted this outcome. If they'd been able, obviously they wouldn't be in the shitstorm they were in.

"Who's this?" the young woman at the car asked. She was young, late teens or early twenties, chewing gum and smiling crookedly as she rested a crowbar over one shoulder. Ariana knew intuitively the girl was razorblade dangerous and she almost told the lie again—that he was her brother. Then she remembered Mark pointed the gun at her, screaming insanity in her ear, and she said, "I don't know. He forced me to drive him at gunpoint."

The woman cocked an eyebrow. "Oh, yeah?"

Ariana did nothing when the young woman dragged Mark from the car. He didn't seem to know what was happening at first, clearly too dazed and emotionally wrecked to comprehend much of anything. He just let himself be pulled, silently, without protest, and then shoved down into the street, landing on his hands and knees.

"Why's he dressed like that?" the woman asked.

"He was a patient in the psych ward."

"Really?" This seemed to intrigue the woman quite a bit. "Fucking nutjob, huh?" She planted a booted foot on Mark's ass and shoved hard, causing him to face plant against the asphalt. He yelped, showing the first signs of fear, as if he was just waking up from a dream to find himself in a nightmare.

"I'm not crazy," he cried, struggling to get up. The woman kicked him hard in the side and he fell over, holding his gut. *"I have stitches!"* He began to cry again and Ariana didn't know how she should feel about that. Should she feel pity? Guilt? Satisfaction?

"Oh, you have stitches?" the woman asked. A car came down the road and she looked up defiantly at it, daring the driver to do anything at all. The car weaved around the scene without so much as slowing down. She turned her attention back to Mark. "Why do you have stitches?"

"My . . . my wife. She . . . stabbed me."

"Stabbed you, huh? Why would your own wife stab you, buddy?"

"I . . . I don't know." Mark coughed, snot and blood dribbling down his chin.

"You don't know." The woman began walking in a circle around his prone body, like a panther toying with a wounded deer. "I don't think I believe that." She paused, snapping her gum. "What's your name?"

He hesitated, until she made to kick him again and then he whined, "Please! It's Mark. My name is Mark. Don't hurt me again."

Ariana was disgusted. He had to be the most pathetic excuse for a man she'd ever encountered. She considered going over there and kicking him herself.

"Hey."

She turned to see Jaclyn staring at her with concern. "Yeah?"

"Not sure I'm digging that look on your face, babe. What are you thinking?"

Ari almost told her the truth but then . . . didn't. She shook her head. "Nothing."

"Well, *Mark*," the young woman said. "My name is Nicki and I'll be your waitress tonight." She laughed. "You wish. Let me rephrase. I'll be your executioner tonight."

Mark wailed and attempted to crawl away, which earned him another kick in the side.

"Stop," Jaclyn yelled, pulling away from Ariana.

Nicki looked at her, annoyance and amusement mingling on her face. "Yeah, that's not gonna happen." She kicked him in the face to prove her point. Mark covered his head with his arms, moaning.

"You're being fucking sadistic!" Jaclyn said. "You're gonna kill him!"

"Exactly," Nicki told her. "I believe I made that clear already. It's just a matter of how long I want to take."

Jaclyn took another step towards her and Nicki brandished the crowbar. "You don't want to interfere, believe me."

Jaclyn looked back at Ariana. "We can't let this happen!"

Ariana felt torn. She knew just yesterday, she would have been horrified at the prospect of watching any kind of violence taking place, much less in front of her eyes and unprovoked. But now she'd heard the news and understood the rage. She had heard the things Mark had said when he'd been screaming; whether he thought he was yelling at her or his wife was irrelevant. He'd been expressing his true feelings, as was often the case with anger, despite so many people trying to backpedal that fact once they'd calmed down.

"You heard the shit in the car," Ariana said. "He hates women."

"That's not—"

Nicki interrupted them. "All men hate women," she said. "Whether they admit it or not, and more and more men *are* admitting now, in case you haven't been paying attention. But even the ones who say they don't? They're full of shit. And you want to know why?" She kicked Mark again, maybe for emphasis. "They think we should fuck them how, when and wherever they want. They're pissed we just walk around with these pussies, something they want so fucking bad."

"What?" Jaclyn frowned, incredulous. "That's ridiculous. Not all men think that way."

"Naïve much?" Nicki asked. "Hell, why do you think so many fathers fuck their daughters? Because they don't want those girls to share their pussies with anyone else. Men think pussies are property, like shoes or a watch, and they should be free to them whenever they like. Like air."

"What kind of men have you been hanging

around?" Jaclyn asked, taking yet another step closer. "My father never laid a hand on me or anyone else."

"You're a liar," Nicki said. "And even if you're not, you're exceptionally lucky. All men are trash. Isn't that right, Mark?"

Mark said nothing, curled into a ball, shivering in the street.

"That's right, sister!" someone shouted from behind them. Ariana turned and saw two women crossing a lawn, coming towards them. One of them held a rolling pin in one hand. "The worm had *turned*!"

Nicki laughed again as Ariana watched the women. She didn't turn back again until Jaclyn shouted *"NO!"*

When Ariana looked, Nicki was bringing the crowbar down on Mark's skull once, twice and then a third time, cracking it open like a fucking egg.

Jaclyn let out something between a cry and a gasp, grabbing Ariana and burying her face in Ari's neck but Ariana couldn't look away. She was stunned that Mark, despite part of his brain being visible to the world, didn't die.

The women who'd just joined them began whooping and hollering, reminding Ariana of a retirement party she'd once attended for a woman she used to work with. Male strippers had been hired and the women had cheered them on in the same way these women were cheering the murder of an unarmed man in the street of a raging city.

Mark somehow turned his head, seeming to look in her direction, but Ariana could tell he wasn't seeing anything and then his body began to convulse and she finally had to look away.

24

Nicki was the center of attention and she was loving every second of it. She was less thrilled when a splinter of skull pierced her face, just beneath her left eye, but she merely pulled out the bone shard and continued mashing the man's head into something resembling red and white pudding, ignoring the blood that trickled down her face. When there wasn't enough of its skull to smash, she started in on the body. She'd already gotten it into her mind that she didn't want to leave it with a single unbroken bone and she meant to accept the challenge, though it was only in her head. Even when her shoulders began to burn with the effort and she knew she'd pay for this tomorrow, still she raised the crowbar and brought it down again and again with every ounce of her strength. Every crack sent a shiver of pleasure through her, body and soul. She felt she'd finally found her purpose in life.

The two women who'd emerged from the crashed car refused to watch the show and this irritated Nicki to some degree. She was doing them a favor, after all, and it would take women like herself—strong women, unafraid to get their hands dirty—who would ultimately protect the weaker women in this new world, and whether they were physically weaker or just mentally weaker didn't matter. Nicki thought they should get used to showing appreciation now, before they came across a less forgiving woman. Or, worse still, a group of them.

When the women began to walk away, Nicki stopped pulverizing the body and called after them. "Where are you two going?" They ignored her, which annoyed her further, so she walked briskly to catch up to them. "I asked you a question."

They stopped, the tall one, Jac, gazing at her with dull eyes. "What do you care?"

Nicki shrugged and snapped her gum. "I don't. But you're gonna need protection, you know. If you think the animals are all gonna take the uprising lying down, you're gonna get a nasty surprise."

They'd all moved to the sidewalk by then, with the additional two women standing nearby, watching the interaction. Nicki regarded them with interest for a second. The one with the rolling pin nodded at her and she nodded back. "How's the one strapped to the table?"

"Oh," the woman said, waving her free hand dismissively. "He died. Fucking wimp."

"We should all stick together," Nicki said. "All five of us. Safely in numbers and all."

"That's a good idea," the rolling pin woman said. "My name is Nancy and that's Suzy" She jerked her thumb at the other woman, who waved noncommittally.

Nicki looked back at the other two. "I know you're Jac," she said. "Who're you?"

The short one's eyes were brighter but not by much. "Ariana."

"Well, Jac and Ariana, I'm advising you to come with me." She looked at Nancy. "Can we go inside your house for a bit?"

"Hell, yeah," Nancy said. "The more the merrier. We even have beer, if you're thirsty."

Jac and Ariana made no move to follow as Nancy and Suzy headed back to the house again.

Staring hard at Jac, Nicki said, "It would be a shame if something happened to you out there."

"Are you kidding me?" Jac said, new life sparking in her dull eyes. "Did you actually just say that? Do you think we're in a fucking movie right now? Are you a gangster?"

Nicki looked down at the gore dripping off the crowbar, then made eye contact again. "I could be."

"So, you're threatening us?"

The street light they stood under suddenly blinked out. They looked around to see the entire street was dark—maybe the entire city.

Nancy, almost at the front door, turned back to them and yelled, "Woo! *Now* it's a party!"

"Fuck," Ariana muttered, clasping Jac's hand in hers.

That was the moment Nicki realized they were lovers, not friends, not sisters, not cousins. Lovers. She smiled. "I'm not threatening you. I'm doing the opposite. *Men* are the threat and they always have been. They're monsters and now no one is holding them accountable. More so than ever before. You should come into the house for you own safety."

"I think we'll take our chances," Jac said, starting to walk away once more, still clasping Ariana's hand. But Ariana stayed rooted to where she was, glancing between her girlfriend and Nicki.

"I don't know, Jaclyn," she said. "Maybe she's right."

About four blocks away, something exploded, startling them all with a tremendous boom, the sky brightening with firelight and huge plumes of black smoke.

They all stood watching the sky for a long moment before Nicki asked, "You still think you want to take your chances out there?"

Jaclyn regarded her with disdain. "You'd never be able to protect anyone from something like that.

170

Not even yourself."

More cars drove by, steering around both the accident and the dead body. No one stopped. The drivers barely slowed their vehicles, probably on their way to flee the city entirely.

"Of course not," Nicki agreed. "But together we can keep the fuckers away. No one will get close enough to do anything like that."

"You can't know that," Jaclyn said.

"Okay, whatever." Nicki was growing bored. There would be other women to come along, grateful for the opportunity to group up with others for protection. "Suit yourselves." She started to walk away, then stopped, and reversed direction again. She passed Jaclyn and Ariana, headed for their car.

"What are you doing?" Ariana asked.

Nicki crawled into the car, ignoring the question. She put the crowbar on the backseat and then began searching the floorboards. She found the gun almost immediately. Satisfied, she grabbed the crowbar again and got out of the car, offering the two women a smile as she passed. "Good luck out there."

"Wait!" Ariana said.

"Nope," Nicki said. "Go if you want or stay if you want but I'm not waiting for shit."

She heard Ariana whispering frantically to Jaclyn but she didn't bother trying to decipher the whispers. She was beginning to think these particular women would be useless anyway. They had, after all, been harboring one of *them*.

Nancy had left the door open and when Nicki entered the house, the kitchen was on the right. Nancy was lighting candles near the sink while Suzy used a Mag-Lite to examine the corpse still bent over the table. Probably the same flashlight they'd raped it with, Nicki thought with some distaste, hoping Darlene had at least washed it.

Nicki walked up beside Suzy and stood beside her, also checking out the body. Now, instead of blood running down its legs, she saw the gore streaking its ass as well. The legs were almost entirely red and a veritable lake of blood congealed on the floor beneath it. Blood still trickled from the black, gaping maw that had once been its asshole. The insides of the ass cheeks were abraded, angry and raw, spread wide in a way Nicki had never witnessed and would never have thought possible if not for the fact she was looking right at it.

"You really did a number on this one," she said with admiration.

"Thanks," Suzy smiled, admiring the corpse as if it were a masterpiece.

"Husband?" Nicki asked.

"Not mine," Suzy said. "Somebody's though. And Nancy's uncle."

Across the room, Nancy blew out a match. "He was a handsy fucker. Got to me when I was about fifteen but there were others in my family too. An aunt and cousin and those are just the ones I know about."

"Fuck." Nicki shook her head, repulsed. "I'm glad justice was finally served."

"And this is just the beginning," Suzy said, grinning. "Our time has finally come."

"Hell, yeah, it has," Nicki agreed, returning the smile. She felt the tingle of excitement again. Electricity coursing through her body in a way Christmas morning had never done. "With any luck, we'll make every last one of these fuckers pay."

"We have the numbers," Nancy said as she brought a candle over to the table. The golden glow of firelight showed her eyes sparkling with delight. "We'll lose some, sure, but we've been losing since the dawn of time. We're used to it. They aren't."

Suzy nodded at the corpse. "That's why we need to get this fucker outside and why it needed to be so brutal. Sexual violence is the threat they've always used and it's what they understand best. Once they see we're just as capable of committing such atrocities and that none of them are safe . . . " She trailed off, laughing a little.

Nancy finished her thought for her. "The world is ours."

25

A second explosion rocked the night, causing Ariana to shudder and tighten her grip on Jaclyn's hand. "We can't stay out here."

"I agree," Jaclyn said. "But, you saw what that chick did to Mark. She's a fucking psychopath. I mean, *look at him*! There's practically nothing left! There's no way he'll even be able to be identified!"

Ariana didn't look at him. She'd never get the image out of her head and didn't need to see it again. "I know. I get it. But, don't you think it's better to be on her good side? I'd rather have her as a friend than an enemy."

"Why do we have to have her as either? I say we just find another place to hide until this shit all blows over."

Ariana couldn't believe what she was hearing.

"Jac," she said, slowly. "This isn't going to blow over. Not for a long time anyway. And think about it—do you really want everything to go back to the way it was before? With men ruling literally everything and treating women as fucking chattel? Perpetrating violence whenever they feel like it, just because they can? You want to continue to be unable to walk the streets at night because men are a threat? To always second guess if you should be alone with this or that guy? It was no way to live and men were never going to change. Even the ones who agreed with us were never willing to do anything about it. They were always too scared of fucking offending other men and didn't give a shit how that presented themselves to women. They talked the talk but were never willing to walk the walk and if they haven't yet, they never will."

"So, what? We just *murder* them all?"

"Of course not. That would be . . . " Ariana stopped. What *would* that be? Impossible? Inhumane? "I just . . . I don't know. Think the herd could use culling, I guess."

Jaclyn stared at her, disbelieving.

Knowing she'd said too much, or maybe not said it well enough, Ariana quickly added, "I'm not talking about mass graves here, Jac. I don't personally want to hurt anyone—"

"You just want them to do it?" Jaclyn interrupted, pointing at the house Nicki had gone into.

"No. No, no. I just think we can only benefit from men being afraid for a change. This whole thing started because they cover for each other. Male lawyers, male judges, all protecting these guys who commit horrible, heinous crimes. You have to see how it emboldens them. Nothing gets better. It only gets worse. Women are prey to these monsters. Wouldn't it be amazing if that mentality stopped?"

A pickup truck drove slowly up the road and they both turned to look at it. All the other traffic had been speeding by, the drivers in a hurry to get wherever they were going, but this driver was doing the opposite. It slowed to a crawl as it came up to the scene of the accident, finally stopping, its headlights illuminating the body in the street.

The person in the passenger seat leaned out the window, shining a flashlight on the corpse, moving the beam back and forth. In the backlight, it was obvious to Ariana the passenger was male but he'd yet to spot her and Jaclyn, masked as they were by total darkness.

"Holy shit," the guy said. "This just happened." The driver said something inaudible in response and the passenger shone the flashlight towards the buildings on his side of the car. The light fell on Ariana and Jaclyn a moment later and froze there. "Winner, winner, chicken dinner," the passenger said. He tossed open the door and stepped out of the truck while something flashed within it. The guy kept his light trained on them. "Evening, ladies."

It was hard to tell exactly what he looked like, but it was clear he was a larger man sporting a beard and wearing a light-colored flannel shirt and a baseball cap.

"What happened here?" he asked. He sounded casual but Ariana knew he wasn't expecting an answer. Certainly not one that would satisfy him. Behind him, he'd left the pickup truck door open and he turned back to it briefly and it was then that Ariana realized what the strange flashing, flickering light within the truck cab was. The guy spun back around, a flaming bottle now in his free hand. "Think quick, cunts," he called as he threw the Molotov cocktail at them. Though they were already in motion and turning away, it smashed mere feet to Jaclyn's right, dousing her lower right leg with burning alcohol.

She screamed as Ariana pulled her away towards the house where Nicki had gone. Ari knew she couldn't stop to put out the flames because a glance over her shoulder showed her the man was getting yet another Molotov from the driver, preparing to hit them with another, probably more accurately thrown, bottle.

"Come on!" Ariana shouted. Jaclyn didn't need any coaxing. They both ran as fast as they could across the lawn and towards the front door, which stood open to the night.

Nicki and Suzy stepped outside just as Ari and

Jac were arriving at the bottom of the front steps and for one horrifying moment, Ariana thought they were going to bar the passage to safety. They didn't. Instead, they quickly stepped aside allowing them to pass through the threshold, where Nancy waited holding a thick wool blanket to put out the flames crawling up Jaclyn's leg. Just on the other side of the doorway, Suzy lifted a rifle and fired at the truck while Nicki fired the gun she'd retrieved from Ariana's car.

Another Molotov flew at them but neither woman seemed particularly fazed, as it landed several yards in front of them. Instead of fleeing, they continued to fire their weapons. The man throwing the bottles shouted something and Ari could only hope he'd been hit but then he was jumping back inside the truck and it roared off down the road, tires squealing as it gave the car accident a wide berth.

"*Better run, fuckers!*" Nicki yelled after them, but she sounded more amused than angry.

"I think you hit him," Suzy said as they entered the house once more.

"Sure hit that fucking truck," Nicki said, closing the door behind herself and turning the bolt.

Jaclyn lay on the floor of the foyer, the blanket over her leg, sweat pouring down her face as Ariana knelt beside her.

"You're gonna have to take those pants off," Nancy said. "See how bad you're burned."

178

"No!" Jaclyn snapped. "I . . . can't."

"You have to," Nancy countered. She knelt on the other side of Jaclyn and began to pull the blanket back.

"*No*," Jaclyn cried, gripping the blanket tightly.

"Just . . . give her a minute," Ariana said.

Nancy didn't say anything for a moment and Ariana saw a hardness in the older woman's eyes. Long before this night, Nancy had seen more than her fair share of shit. Finally, Nancy said, "Okay, but I wouldn't wait longer than a minute or so. The fabric will stick, if it's not already, and then you're really gonna be in a world of hurt." She stood up and walked into the kitchen with Suzy and Nicki. From the foyer, Ariana could see the corpse of the naked man strapped to the table, his lower body drenched with drying blood, and she grimaced, looking away quickly.

"She's right, you know," Ariana said to Jaclyn. "We're gonna need to look at those burns."

Jaclyn winced. "I'm scared to look."

"You don't have to. I'll look. It might not be as bad as you think, but we need to check it out."

After a moment, Jaclyn bit her lower lip and nodded, tears streaming down her cheeks. She finally released the blanket and Ariana pulled it down. "Can we get some light over here?" she said to the women in the kitchen.

Nancy stepped into the foyer and bent down

once more, the flashlight in one hand and a large pair of kitchen shears in the other. She handed the light to Ariana. To Jaclyn, she said, "I'm gonna start cutting from the bottom, okay? First let's take off that shoe."

Trembling, Ariana held the flashlight as still as she was able. Unlike Jaclyn, however, she shook not with fear, but with rage.

26

At the kitchen window, Nicki gazed out at the night, watching the street. She'd put her weapons on the counter, though they were within easy reach if need be. She was proud of herself for firing the gun at the monsters in the truck, as she'd never fired one before. There hadn't been much to it though. It was a small caliber without much kick and though she didn't kid herself about her ability with the weapon, she was convinced she'd done decently and thought she'd do even better next time. And she knew there would be a next time, probably before the night was over and if not, certainly in the coming days.

Behind her in the foyer, she heard Jaclyn howl in pain. Nothing too extreme—she wasn't wailing—but it was clear she was hurting. Nicki hoped it was nothing too debilitating, as they'd probably need her in the not too distant future. She assumed Nancy would clean the burns, probably use a salve and dress the leg.

Suzy joined her at the window and draped an arm over Nicki's shoulder while peeking out the blind with her free hand. Nicki yawned and Suzy followed suit. It was the first time Nicki felt truly tired. She said, "I think I'm gonna need to crash for a couple hours. I'm dead."

Chuckling, Suzy said, "Not yet you're not but you might be soon enough. Dead, that is. We'll probably all be dead before this is done."

"You think so?" The idea didn't scare Nicki as much as she would have thought.

"Maybe." Suzy didn't seem particularly bothered by the notion either. Maybe they were both resigned to it. "But, I agree. You should go upstairs and catch some Z's if you can. I think we should sleep in shifts until this all shakes out, one way or another."

Nicki looked at her. "Shakes out?"

"Yeah. Eventually, the National Guard or the Marines will drop the hammer on all this. I don't know if they'll be able to suss out who did what and even if they do, it'll probably take years, but when they come, it won't be pretty."

"We can fight them."

Suzy smiled sadly. "We'll lose."

"Does it matter? I think the fighting is what's important."

"You're right. It *is* important. What's happened here will have long-lasting effects. Future generations will learn about it and anyone who wants to treat women like shit will think twice about it for a long-ass time, knowing we can be as brutal as them."

They fell silent. Somewhere in the distance, they could hear gunfire. Nicki hoped another monster was being slain. Even one less would make the world a better, safer place. She yawned again. "Okay, I'm gonna go find a place to rest for a little while. Don't let me sleep long."

"You got it, sister."

Nicki grabbed a candle and the crowbar but left the gun where it was, just in case it was needed while she slept, then she made her way through the house.

Jaclyn now lay on the sofa in the living room, one pant let sheared off high on her thigh, the leg wrapped in gauze. Nancy was dumping a couple of pills into Jaclyn's right hand, presumably Tylenol or something similar. Ariana sat nearby in a chair, her face lit by candlelight. She looked haggard, like a woman on the verge of a nervous breakdown.

"I'm gonna crash for a bit," Nicki told them as she passed through. "Make sure I'm up in a few hours."

"Make yourself at home," Nancy said. "Spare room is at the end of the hall on the right. Bed is freshly made."

Nicki thanked her and wearily climbed the stairs, already knowing just a few hours would not be enough to refresh her. She couldn't remember the last time she'd felt this beat.

She found the guest room and closed the door, setting the candle down on the nightstand and laying on top of the covers. She knew if she got beneath them, she'd be too comfortable and difficult to rouse. As an afterthought, she swallowed her gum. On more than one occasion, she'd fallen asleep with it in her mouth only to wake up with it stuck in her hair.

On her back, she stared at the dancing shadows on the ceiling caused by the flickering flame nearby. Outside, the night sounded alternately completely silent or, just moments later, like a warzone. She wondered again if her boss had survived the clubbing she'd given him and how Marge and Shirley were faring. She suspected she would never see Marge again and wasn't sure how she felt about that. She realized now how little they'd ever had in common. She remembered too the female officer in the street and hoped she was still out there, fighting the good fight, fucking up as many monsters as she could. Nicki wished she'd been able to jump into that squad car with the woman and imagined patrolling the night with her, shooting down every monster unlucky enough to cross their path. The fantasy made her smile in the dark room and she closed her eyes, almost regretful she had to sleep.

Ten minutes later, shouting roused her and she sat straight up, glancing at her watch to discover it hadn't been ten minutes at all, but ninety. She could hardly believe her eyes but swung her legs off the bed, head cocked, alert and listening.

It hadn't been a dream. Downstairs, someone shouted her name again. She snatched the crowbar from where she'd placed it on the dresser and ran from the room, bounding down the stairs two at a time.

Back in the kitchen, she found Nancy at the window, peering out, rifle in hand. "Those fuckers are back," Nancy told her. "And they brought friends."

When Nicki looked out, she saw the same dark-colored pickup truck from earlier, along with an oversized SUV. Four shadowy heads stuck up on the far side of the vehicles, ready to duck down if they saw the need.

"Come out," a gruff male voice shouted towards the house. "Or we'll come in."

"How long have they been out there?" Nicki asked.

"About two minutes. Luckily, I was already keeping watch."

"Where are the others?"

"Ariana is in the master bedroom, keeping an eye on the backyard and Suzy went down to the basement with your gun in case they try to come in that way."

"Jaclyn?"

"Living room. She couldn't get upstairs to be with

her lady. I doubt she'll be much use if these pricks try to get in. Last resort, maybe. I gave her a knife from the block but she's pretty out of it."

Nicki looked around. "Maybe we should blow out the candles?"

"They already know we're in here."

"Yeah, but if we blow them out, our eyes will adjust to the dark but when they come in, they'll be blind."

Nancy glanced at her, impressed. "Good thinking. Hurry."

Nicki jogged through the house extinguishing all the candles. She got to the basement and told Suzy to put out the flashlight she'd placed on the floor, explaining her theory. Upstairs, she found Ariana at the bedroom window, remaining more stoic than Nicki would have imagined.

"Do you think they're gonna come in?" Ariana asked.

"I think they're gonna try."

Back downstairs, she took up position near the front door in the foyer. Nancy was to her left, Jaclyn to her right. She hefted the weight of the crowbar in her hands. It felt good. Better than good.

It felt righteous.

27

Ariana didn't like leaving Jaclyn downstairs and was deeply regretting coming into this house in the first place. The fact they were now stuck here, under siege, felt entirely like her fault and she debated just going outside to explain to these rampaging men that she and Jac were not the ones who'd murdered Mark in the street, had in fact, tried to prevent it, but she doubted they would listen or believe her. They'd probably kill her before she even got a single word out of her mouth and besides, what if somehow they *did* let her and Jaclyn go and then proceeded to enter the house and murder the rest of the women within? Could she live with that? Because it sure as shit would happen.

She knew it didn't matter now, as the men in the street, hiding behind their vehicles and shouting at the house, were almost certainly scared out of their minds of the way things were going. They didn't want to talk reason any more than Nicki and the other women here did. They all wanted war and she and Jac were now caught in the middle.

"Not gonna ask again, bitches," the ringleader outside shouted. "Get your sweet tits out here or we're coming in! No more mister nice guy!"

Ariana doubted he'd ever been a nice guy. He was probably an MRA. Maybe he wasn't scared at all. Maybe he and his friends were excited, finally able to slaughter some women without consequence. Maybe this was the day they'd all been dreaming about, posting online about, bragging to each other about when they shared their violent fantasies with each other. It was men like them who'd made Ariana get off social media in the first place. They shouted from the rooftops about "feminism is cancer" but it was they themselves who were causing women to hate men more and more frequently. Nicki was a perfect example—a straight woman who'd heard and witnessed too much shit to ever fully trust men again; and to think, it was always lesbians getting flack for being "men haters," when in reality, straight women had far more cause to be disgruntled with the male population than gay women did. Straight women were the ones who were cheated on, abandoned, often with children and for younger women, physically and sexually abused by husbands and boyfriends, disrespected in their relationships, by their fathers, brothers, co-workers. The list went on and on. In truth, it was miraculous the showdown sweeping the world now hadn't happened much sooner, even decades ago.

The sound of a gunshot snapped Ariana out of her thoughts, and she focused once more on the activity outside.

No heads were popping up from behind the vehicles and she suspected it was Nancy who'd fired, perhaps as a warning. Her suspicions were confirmed a second later when she heard the woman shout, "You assholes need to find someone else to harass or you're not gonna live long! We're armed to the teeth in here!"

The last sentence made Ariana wince. She didn't think anyone who was, in fact, well-armed would feel the need to announce it and she thought the threat would ring false to the men outside as well.

What she didn't expect was more gunfire.

The men crouched behind the SUV popped up with their own firearms and began shooting at the house. The sound was tremendous and the rounds were hitting the lower half of the house. She ducked down and away from the window. The only weapon she had was an aluminum baseball bat Nancy had supplied her with—obviously no match for firearms.

The men fired approximately twenty rounds into the house before stopping. The ringleader shouted,

"Last chance, bitches!"

Everything was silent and Ariana trembled in fear. Had any of the bullets hit anyone? Was Nancy okay? Jaclyn? Ariana hadn't heard any cries of pain but she knew that didn't necessarily mean anything.

She poked her head over the windowsill to peek down at the street again. Once more, the men had gone into cover behind their vehicles.

Instead of doing as commanded by Nancy, she crept away from the window and didn't stand fully upright until she had left the room and gone into the hallway. At the top of the stairs, she hissed, "Jac! You okay?"

There was a long moment of silence in which Ariana's heart stopped, but then Jaclyn replied, "Yeah, I'm good. Pretty much all the windows are shot out though."

Ducking, Nancy came to the bottom of the stairs. Even in the gloom and from above, Ariana could see the older woman's face was bleeding from multiple gashes. "I told you to keep an eye out up there!"

"Why?" Ariana asked. "I don't have anything to shoot with!"

Nancy wiped blood from her forehead to prevent the stream from dripping into her eye. "Fine. We can—"

Another round of gunfire exploded into the lower level of the house. Nancy hit the floor as Ariana took cover around the wall at the top of the stairs.

She hesitated for only a second before returning to the window in the bedroom, quickly peeking out at the street. What she saw froze her blood.

The two men hiding behind the SUV were laying down cover fire for the other men from the pickup, who were advancing on the house, burning Molotov cocktails in hand.

"Fuck!"

No longer afraid of being shot in the back, Ariana rose and ran from the room, shouting, *"Jaclyn! We have to get out!"* As she reached the bottom step, a burning bottle flew through the shattered window, igniting the curtains instantly. It was as though the electricity had suddenly been restored, the room brightening, the firelight illuminating everything. Jaclyn was on the far side of the sofa, furthest away from the window and Ariana ran to her.

"Where the fuck is Nicki?" Nancy screamed, still on the floor.

Suzy came bounding up the basement stairs, her face stricken with panic as she saw the living room burning.

Ariana struggled to get Jaclyn to her feet while simultaneously attempting to keep them low to avoid the bullets still slamming into the walls and furniture around them.

"Where's Nicki?" Nancy repeated, beginning to sound frantic.

"She went out the basement door," Suzy said.

"Took her gun back too!"

"Goddammit!" Nancy was more enraged than scared.

Another Molotov crashed through a window, this time in the kitchen, setting the body still bound to the table ablaze. It was immediately followed by a second one thrown through the living room window, igniting both an arm chair and the sofa.

We are gonna die, Ariana thought. *We're gonna burn alive.*

Someone outside began pounding on the front door. It sounded as though one of the men were kicking it to get inside. Probably one of the ones with a gun.

"Out the back," Ariana gasped, as the lower level of the house began to fill with black smoke. She had Jaclyn's left arm around her own neck and together they shuffled as quickly as possible to the basement stairs. *"Come on!"*

They'd begun the descent when the front door flew open and Ari glanced back to see not one of the two gunmen, but both. They seemed startled to find Nancy and Suzy just feet from the open door but they didn't hesitate: they raised their weapons and fired at them both, each at nearly point blank range.

Terrified, Ariana faced forward again but lost her footing. Both she and Jaclyn fell down the wooden basement stairs. Ari felt a rib crack before smacking her head hard on the concrete floor at the bottom.

The world swam as she fought to remain conscious. She heard Jaclyn cry out and was dimly aware of her girlfriend landing on top of her. They both grunted in pain and Ariana did her best to crawl out from under Jaclyn's weight. She began coughing, her chest aching from smoke inhalation. Again, her surroundings went in and out of focus, but she refused to let the darkness claim her. She wriggled out from under Jaclyn and managed to get to her feet, pulling Jac up with her, both choking and gagging. On the floor above, more shots rang out and Ariana hoped against hope Nancy was getting off a couple, though she'd seen with her own eyes the other woman take at least two bullets before she'd turned away. The likelihood of Nancy or Suzy still being alive was next to nothing.

Dragging Jaclyn, she made it across the basement to the backdoor, fighting with the deadbolt briefly, though it seemed like ages, before finally pulling it open and feeling the cool night air on her face. She took deep breaths and burst into tears of relief, surprising herself, mostly because the ordeal wasn't over and she knew it, but at least they wouldn't burn to death in a stranger's house.

Instead, she thought wryly, they would probably be shot or just burned alive by a Molotov launched by a homicidal maniac who thought of them as witches to be banished by flame.

28

Knowing she would move faster alone, Nicki didn't bother to tell the others her plan once the monsters began firing at the house. She simply left her position by the front door and went down to the basement to find Suzy peering out the backdoor at the empty backyard. Nicki understood why Nancy had assigned someone to watch the rear entrance but now it seemed pointless.

"Let me have the gun," Nicki said, holding out her hand.

Suzy looked at her, uncertain. "I need it in case they come around."

"They're not coming around. They're coming straight through the front door."

"But . . . Nancy said—"

"It doesn't matter what Nancy said. Just give it

to me."

Upstairs, they heard glass shatter and a low *whooshing* sound. Suzy blinked, showing the first signs of real fear.

"*Give it to me*," Nicki repeated. When Suzy still didn't do as asked, Nicki used her free hand and snatched the pistol away.

"*Hey!*" Suzy cried.

"Trust me," Nicki said and exited the house, hearing Suzy throw the deadbolt behind her.

With so much commotion happening in the front, she was certain no one would notice her crossing the back yard to enter the neighboring backyard. She traveled to the far side of the second house, rounding the corner and making her way to the street, where she paused, hunching down between two parked cars. She peeked out to see two of the monsters advancing on the house where the women were, another round of flaming bottles in hand. She watched them pitch the Molotovs through the broken windows and the other men, the ones with the guns, come out from behind the SUV and charge across the lawn. She ducked down when she thought one of them turned his face towards her, but then heard as they began trying to kick the door in, reassuring her she hadn't been spotted. Or, if she had, they didn't care enough to come after her, maybe because they didn't think she'd come from the house they were focused on. The monsters had only seen Ariana and

195

Jaclyn earlier, which was a good thing for Nicki.

After another quick peek assured her their attention was diverted, she ran across the street and again hid between cars parked on the shoulder of the road before circling around to a vehicle's far side. She figured if they could use cars as cover, so could she.

Peering over the hood with most of her body shielded, she leaned the crowbar against the car and attempted to level the pistol at the monsters with the Molotovs. She scowled down the sight. Even with the added benefit of the firelight to guide her shot, she wasn't so sure she could make it from such a distance. Confidence wavering, she nevertheless knew she had to try. Her finger tightened on the trigger, and then a feminine voice whispered in her ear, *"Don't."*

The voice startled her, causing her to reflexively squeeze the trigger, though the shot went wild and into the night sky. She instantly ducked down behind the car, hoping the monsters across the street were too engrossed in the slaughter of innocent women to hear the weapon's discharge.

The woman beside her, also crouching behind the car, was, like Nicki herself, barely out of her teens, though she was dark-haired and petite, and holding what Nicki thought of as serious firepower. An AK-47, maybe? She wasn't good with guns, but it looked to her like the kind of weapon soldiers used on the battlefield. The kind so many male mass shooters favored.

Holding an index finger to her lips, the young woman then pointed to the house nearest them. Shadows moved swiftly in the side yards, stopping in deepest shadows and behind trees. Nicki looked at the woman questioningly. The woman then made a circle motion, her finger pointed skyward. Nicki understood the gesture to mean, *all around us.*

"There are women in that house!" Nicki hissed. "They're going to kill them!"

"Probably already have," the woman confirmed.

They both raised their heads over the hood of the car to see the house across the street now engulfed in flames. Fire showed in every window on the lower level and Nicki felt fury rising in her heart. *"Mother-fuckers,"* she snarled.

It was as if the word was magic, bringing forth the army of shadows. Out of the darkness stepped over a dozen women bearing an abundance of weaponry. Nicki's eyes widened as the women marched forward, their strides full of purpose, weapons aimed. Several of them moved past the car Nicki hid behind and into the street. When those with guns began firing, Nicki dropped her own pistol to cover her ears.

She watched as the monsters with their flaming bottles dropped, their heads exploded into, in the strange light, what almost appeared to be more dust than mist, fire spreading like living puddles on the lawn around them. The small army of women kept moving toward the burning house and when one of the pricks, drawn by the noise outside, poked his head around the doorjamb to peer at the oncoming forces, he too was shot immediately, his body falling out of sight.

The smoke from the burning structure was drifting across to where Nicki stood and she began coughing. Tears sprang from her eyes and she attempted to clear her throat, which caused her to cough harder. Vision blurry, she questioned what she saw next: more silhouettes emerging from the deepest pits of gloom, including some of the surrounding homes. From the body types, Nicki assumed they were all female.

More and more women poured into the street, some cautious at first, but growing bolder with every step, sensing the now unstoppable reckoning. Squinting, Nicki saw figures round the back corner of Nancy's house, one leaning on the other, as they ran in her direction and she knew she was looking at Ariana and Jaclyn. Nicki had mixed feelings upon seeing they'd survived both the fire and the gunshots. On one hand, they'd protected that monster Mark, shielding the enemy and forcing her to do their dirty work, but on the other, they were women and based on that alone, sisters-in-arms.

She stooped, searching for the dropped pistol while cheers of victory pierced the night, rolling off the houses and foothills like glorious thunder. The war cry of every goddess, because that's what women were—goddesses who survived and would always survive just fine on their own, with no use for the males of the species.

Still coughing, she couldn't find the gun in all the darkness and she wished she'd thought to take a candle or flashlight from Nancy's house. She knelt on the ground, feeling the sidewalk's asphalt with blind fingers, searching, searching .   .   .

29

Ariana spotting Nicki the moment they rounded the back of the house and moved into the side yard. She was standing across the street on the far side of a car, staring at the burning home.

"Come on," Ariana urged. Jaclyn was limping badly but still able to move with decent enough speed. They couldn't run if they needed to, which worried Ariana. "Did you see that?"

Grimacing, Jaclyn nodded and forced herself to move faster. The flames behind them, they crossed the street hurriedly, Ari wondering if an explosion was coming. How bizarre that would be, she thought. Like something out of a movie.

Seconds before they reached Nicki, she dropped down behind the car and Ariana noticed for the first time a couple of dark figures standing on the front stoop of the new house, arms around each other, but she paid them little mind. The chaos around them was intensifying and she could only think about Nicki.

When they rounded the car, Nicki was on the ground, coughing. Ariana let go of Jaclyn, allowing her to lean on the hood of the car and she stooped beside Nicki. "You're okay," she told the younger woman, cradling the back of her head in her hand and pulling Nicki into her own lap. "You're good."

Nicki coughed, the blood bubbling out from between her lips looking black in the darkness but still visible against her pale skin.

"I got you, Nicki," Ariana said, panic knotting in her belly. She lifted Nicki's T-shirt. The hole the automatic weapon had created in her abdomen seemed impossibly huge and black. Ariana placed her palm against the wound, hoping to staunch the blood but she didn't have much hope. "I got you," she repeated. Then inhaled sharply as Nicki coughed up more blood. "Did you see who shot you?"

To Ariana's amazement, Nicki grinned, her teeth smeared with black blood. "Fucking men. Bute're like amazons," Nicki said. "Fuck them, right?"

Ariana, her face puzzled and concerned, looked over at Jaclyn, who could only shake her head.

"So many women now," Nicki continued. "There's no way we can lose the war." She turned her head and her smile broadened further still. Ariana glanced in the direction Nicki was looking but there was nothing there. "I can't believe how loud they're cheering," Nicki said, coughing again. She winced, her eyes rolling into the back of her head for several terrifying seconds before she focused on Ariana's face again. "Tomorrow is gon . . . gonna be . . . awesome."

Ariana had no idea who'd shot Nicki. They'd only seen a shadow approach her from behind. It appeared that the person had said something close to Nicki's ear and then there'd been a loud *pop* and then the person had vanished, running off in the opposite direction from the way Ariana and Jaclyn were coming. If it had been a man or a woman, Ariana couldn't say.

When it looked like Nicki was losing consciousness, Ariana gave her a quick, gentle shake. "Nicki! Stay awake, okay?"

"I'm awake," Nicki said and swallowed loudly. She shivered and Ariana could actually feel the warmth leaving her body. "I . . . " A geyser of blood spewed forth, splashing up into Ariana's face before settling back onto Nicki's, covering it like a red mask. Ariana heard Jaclyn gasp but she didn't dare look away from Nicki's eyes. "I'm as . . . awake . . . as . . . I've ever . . . ev . . . been." She sighed heavily before adding, "I don't . . . feel . . . very good." Her eyes fell away from Ariana's, looking off over her shoulder.

She smiled again, a tiny, heartbreaking smile, before saying, "We . . . we . . . "

Ariana waited. She waited for nearly a full minute before she accepted Nicki's final sentence would never be finished. Then she lay Nicki's head back on the ground and stood up, joining Jaclyn at the car. She wiped the young woman's blood from her own eyes as she and Jaclyn watched the blaze. For the first time, she noticed more people had gathered. Some of them, Ariana noted with a bit of dismay coupled with sour amusement, were recording the event with cellphones.

If the men who'd started the fire had entered the house along with the gunmen, she hadn't seen it and didn't know. Part of her hoped they had. Hoped they'd gone in and were never coming out again.

For the first time in hours, she heard distant sirens again. She wondered if someone had had the presence of mind to call the fire department. She hoped so, though it was clear there would be nothing to save.

A few minutes later, they heard a sound they hadn't heard since the entire shitstorm had begun: rotor blades. Soon, a chopper was in sight. Everyone shielded their eyes, looking skyward as the helicopter hovered above the burning structure. Ariana was disappointed, but not completely surprised, to see it was a news copter rather than any type of rescue vehicle.

Jaclyn scoffed. "Figures."

Ariana was exhausted. She felt dizzy. Maybe from the smoke wafting over to them or maybe because she'd never been so sore and tired in her life, but whatever it was, she needed to get out of here. She had no idea what time it was but could only assume it would be daylight soon.

She wondered about the wreckage of the world and what it would look like in the morning light. How much would there be to salvage? Not enough, she thought. The world had been deeply damaged and would most certainly bear the scars for a long time to come, if people were even finished fucking it up in the first place. She hoped they were but she also doubted it.

We, she mentally corrected herself. *If* we're *finished fucking it up. Not* them. There could be no more *them*, she knew. That kind of thinking had already hurt too many people, ruined things nearly beyond repair, but that would have to be the key word: *nearly*.

Grabbing Jaclyn's hand, she had to shout to be heard over the sound of the chopper, "Think anyone will give us a ride to the hospital?"

"Are you kidding? I fucking *hope* not. Why would you want to go back to that madhouse?"

"Good point," Ariana agreed. "I probably have ointment for your leg at home. Bandages too."

"Or we could stop at the drugstore. There's one

not too far from here."

"Okay."

"They even sell champagne."

Ariana raised an eyebrow. "What do we have to celebrate?"

"I don't know," Jaclyn said. "Not dying?"

She had to agree that was a good thing to celebrate. "We should still find a ride though. I don't want you limping all the way back."

"I'm tougher than you think, Ari."

"Yeah, but I'm not."

"You are."

They had to move around a few of the people gathered on the sidewalk to start in the right direction and they barely flinched when, somewhere off in the distance, more gunfire erupted, shaking the seemingly endless night.

About the Author

Gina Ranalli is the Wonderland Award winning author of nearly twenty books, mostly in the horror and bizarro fiction genres. She lives in Washington State and you can connect with her online at
twitter.com/ginaranalli.

Also From
Madness Heart Press

Broken Nails by Susan Snyder

Exotic Meats and Inedible Objects by Rachel Rodman

just break my heart already. by Chaire Michael Clemons

Salamander Justice by Tamika Johnson

available online at
http://MadnessHeart.Press

ALL MEN ARE TRASH

Lightning Source UK Ltd.
Milton Keynes UK
UKHW021141031221
395039UK00012B/1032